CATS IN THE CASTLE

Mandy shivered and pulled the covers around her. Suddenly, a trickle of fear ran down her spine. Somehow, she felt she wasn't alone.

Mandy held her breath and strained to listen. Pale moonlight streamed through a crack in the curtains, filling the room with a misty silver light. In the soft glow, she could see that there was nothing there. *It's only my imagination*, she tried to convince herself.

She felt a strong urge to sit up. Unable to resist, she pushed herself up onto her elbows and then, as if by a magnet, found her eyes being drawn to the door.

And there, in a pool of moonlight, sat a small ginger-colored cat, staring back at her with enormous green eyes. . . .

Read more spooky Animal Ark™ Hauntings tales

Cats
in
the Castle

Ben M. Baglio

Illustrations by Ann Baum

**Cover illustration by
John Butler**

AN
APPLE
PAPERBACK

T 12236

SCHOLASTIC INC.

New York Toronto London Auckland Sydney
Mexico City New Delhi Hong Kong Buenos Aires

Special thanks to Andrea Abbott

ISBN 0-439-44898-0

12 11 10 9 8 7 6 5 4 3 2   3 4 5 6 7 8/0

Printed in the U.S.A.   40

First Scholastic printing, January 2003

Hauntings

One

"Letter for you, Mandy," said her father, Dr. Adam Hope, as he came into the kitchen with the mail.

Mandy looked at the postmark on the bulky white envelope. "It's from Dorset," she observed, tearing it open.

"Dorset? Who do you know there?" her dad asked.

Mandy shrugged her shoulders as she took out a glossy brochure and its accompanying letter. No one sprang to mind. She unfolded the letter and started to read out loud: *Dear Miss Hope*, she began. Then she stopped abruptly.

"What's up?" Dr. Adam frowned, tugging at his beard.

"I don't believe it! I've won a prize!" Mandy exclaimed.

Eagerly, she read on: *We are delighted to inform you that you have won first prize in our recent "Find the hidden animals in the jungle" contest.* She looked up, her eyes shining. "I'd forgotten I'd entered that contest," she said. "It was at the back of a wildlife magazine we had in the waiting room."

Mandy's mom and dad were vets. They ran a clinic called Animal Ark that was attached to their home in the Yorkshire village of Welford. Mandy loved animals more than anything else in the world and never missed a chance to read the wildlife magazines that people brought to the clinic.

"What have you won?" asked Dr. Emily.

Mandy handed her mother the brochure. "*We* have won a mystery weekend for four at Wardour Castle in Dorset." She grinned.

"A weekend in a castle! That sounds terrific!" said Dr. Emily, looking at the picture of the stately home on the front of the brochure. "It looks like an amazing place," she added.

Mandy nodded. "It says here that after centuries of being a private family home, the castle has now been turned into a luxury hotel."

"Well, you can count me in," said Dr. Emily. She admired the color photo of the marbled entrance hall. "Solving a mystery should be great fun." She turned a page and pointed to a photograph of a man in Edwardian clothes. "It looks like they really get into the spirit of things. Everyone dresses up in costume for dinner."

Mandy grimaced as she pictured herself in a stiff Edwardian dress. "Well, as long as it's not for the whole time," she said.

Dr. Adam chuckled. "Mmm. I can't really see you wandering around in that kind of get-up all weekend." He gave Mandy a hug. "Well done, honey," he said.

Dr. Emily gave the brochure back to Mandy. "Need I ask who the fourth person in our party will be?" she asked, smiling.

Mandy grinned at her. "I'll tell him now," she said as she ran into the hall to phone her best friend, James Hunter.

"I wonder what our mystery will be," pondered Mandy as they drove past the gatehouse at the entrance to Wardour Castle late the following Friday afternoon.

"The unexplained disappearance of all guests aged twelve," joked Dr. Adam, winking at her in the rearview mirror.

"Well, I'll be OK, in that case," said James, who was eleven.

Mandy was about to answer back when they rounded a bend and saw the imposing front of the castle just ahead of them. Set on a hill, the three-storied building dominated the skyline with its dark stone walls and turreted towers.

"Wow!" gasped Mandy. The leaded windows glinted orange in the setting autumn sun, while the rooftop parapet cast odd, notch-shaped shadows on the surrounding lawns. The land sloped away gently to woodland on one side and fields on the other. At one end of the castle stood a squat, square tower with uneven buttressed walls.

"I bet the really creepy parts of the mystery will happen in there," said James, pointing.

"Ah, yes, the keep," said Dr. Adam. "Probably the oldest part of the castle." Then, with a theatrical wobble to his voice, he added, "An ideal haunting ground for old ghosts! And where they lock up guests or stolen goods."

Mandy laughed and shook her head. "That would be too obvious. I hope the mystery will be a little more interesting than that."

The driveway swept past a formal pond. A glittering cascade of water tumbled into it from an ornate fountain. *Strange*, Mandy thought to herself. The stone fountain looked a lot like a cat, but it was difficult to see for sure with all the water gushing from it.

Dr. Adam pulled up next to several other cars in the graveled parking lot. Mandy and James picked up their backpacks, then made their way toward the vast oak front door, eager to see inside.

Just as they reached the short flight of stone steps leading up to the entrance, the front door swung open and a thin, elderly man appeared, wearing a long black coat and striped gray-and-black trousers.

"Good afternoon," the man said in a voice that was so deep and formal that Mandy found herself thinking of dusty, antique furniture and old, leather-covered books. "You must be the Hopes and Master Hunter."

"That's right," said Dr. Adam, reaching the top of the steps and shaking the old man's outstretched hand.

"My name is Fellows," continued the man. "I'm the butler. If you would be so good as to come this way, please."

"A butler!" Mandy raised her eyebrows.

Before they stepped inside, Mandy looked at a pair of gray stone cats flanking the wide doorway. The tall, lichen-spotted statues looked sternly ahead, as if keeping vigil over the castle grounds. "Nice watchdogs," she joked to James, running a hand down the back of one of them.

"Probably a lot better than Blackie." James laughed as he referred to his Labrador, who had been left at home.

They entered a vast wood-paneled hall that rose up

to a high, vaulted ceiling. Fellows paused briefly while they looked around them, then continued across the foyer, his footsteps ringing out loudly on the black and white tiles.

"More watch cats!" said James, pointing to a row of polished marble cats that stood on pedestals against the back wall.

Mandy nodded appreciatively. "Makes a change from busts of human ancestors," she said, her words echoing in the vast hall.

Fellows led them through an oak-paneled door into a small, welcoming room furnished with comfortable armchairs and a very tidy, businesslike desk next to the window. "The Hope party," he announced formally. Then he turned and left.

A tall woman with long, glossy black hair looked up from her desk. "Welcome to Wardour," she said with a calm smile. She pushed back her chair and came across to them, her high heels clicking sharply on the tile floor. "I'm Mrs. Hapgood — Margaret — your host for the weekend. Would you like to sign the guest book for me, please?"

After Dr. Emily had signed the book and filled in their details, Mrs. Hapgood unhooked two sets of keys from a rack on the wall behind her desk. "I'll show you to your rooms," she said, ushering them back out into the hall. "I'm sure you'll want to freshen up after your long journey." She gestured toward an arched doorway. "The dining room is through here. When you're ready, please join us for lunch." She led them up the sweeping staircase that led to a long, banistered gallery overlooking the entrance hall.

Glancing down, Mandy saw that the black and white tiles below were arranged in a distinct pattern. "It looks like a cat on the prowl," she whispered to James.

"It does," he agreed. "And look, more cats," he said, running his hand over the ornately carved cats' heads on the banisters.

"Those banisters are nearly as old as the castle itself," said Mrs. Hapgood, overhearing them. "Most of the castle has been renovated very recently, of course. We had to do a great deal of work before we could reopen it as a hotel." She set off briskly along a thickly carpeted hallway. "Your rooms are this way."

They followed her past several closed doors. Mandy guessed they must be the doors of other bedrooms. Ahead of them, where the hallway turned sharply, there was a tall window. Heavy gold curtains hung on either side of it.

Drawing nearer, Mandy saw that the drapes were intricately embroidered with gold patterns of cats of all shapes and sizes. "They must really love cats here," she remarked to James. "There are statues or pictures of them everywhere."

Farther down the hall, Mrs. Hapgood had stopped and was unlocking a door. "This is your suite," she said to Mandy's parents. She stood back to allow them to go in.

"It's beautiful!" came Dr. Emily's voice from inside. "What luxury!"

Mandy peered through the door, expecting to find a room full of priceless antiques. "But it's modern!" she exclaimed, disappointed to see an uncluttered, expensively furnished room that could have been found in any popular hotel.

Mrs. Hapgood looked pleased. "It is now. But when I first came here, it looked like something out of a museum!"

"Have you owned hotels before?" asked Dr. Adam. He heaved his suitcase onto the bed and looked appreciatively around the comfortable room.

Mrs. Hapgood shook her head and smiled. "Not exactly. You see, I was living in London until recently. When I learned that I had inherited Wardour from my great-uncle, I moved down here. You can imagine how much it costs to run a castle, so I thought I would open it as a hotel. This is only our second group of guests!" She jangled the other set of keys. "Now," she said, turning to Mandy and James. "Let me show you to your rooms. They're not much farther."

Mrs. Hapgood led them to a gnarled wooden door at the far end of the hall. She turned the key in the heavy brass lock and the door creaked open to reveal a room that looked as if it were straight out of the Dark Ages.

Mandy let out a deep breath. "It's great!" she said, stepping into the room. "It's even got a four-poster bed!"

"Unfortunately, we still have to renovate this room," Mrs. Hapgood explained.

The only window was a narrow barred gap in the wall. It allowed in just enough light for Mandy to notice the pattern on the brocade cushions — more cats.

"It's really creepy!" James said and grinned. "Just like I imagined it would be." He turned to Mrs. Hapgood. "Is mine the same?"

Mrs. Hapgood nodded. "Yes, it is," she said. "It's through there. I hope you like it!" She pointed to a low white door in the back corner of the room and seemed amused at their enthusiasm for the old-fashioned furnishings. As she turned to go, she added, "You'll each find a folder on your bedside table with information about this weekend's mystery. I'll be giving you the first clue at lunch." And, with that, she disappeared back down the hallway.

As Mandy bounced experimentally on the edge of the bed, she tried to conjure up a picture of who might have lived here in the past. It would be interesting to find out some of the history of the castle. Suddenly, a flicker of movement at the foot of the bed caught her eye. She just glimpsed an orange blur before it slipped out of sight under the bed.

"What's that?" she asked, scrambling to her feet.

"I'm not sure," said James, putting down the brochure he had been reading. "I think it looked like a cat."

"So do I," agreed Mandy. "A ginger one."

They knelt down and looked under the bed.

"That's strange," said Mandy. "There's nothing there."

"Maybe it's hiding in the room somewhere," James suggested. He stood up and went over to a small writing desk that was pushed against a wall. He peered behind it, but there was no sign of a cat.

They searched the room for a few minutes, without luck. "It must have sneaked out the door when we weren't looking," said Mandy, checking her watch. "I'm sure we'll see it again somewhere, but right now we'd better think about going down for lunch."

James quickly dusted the knees of his trousers. "Lead the way!" he exclaimed. "I'm starving!"

Dr. Emily, Dr. Adam, and the other guests had already assembled in the dining room when Mandy and James poked their heads around the door.

Mrs. Hapgood was sitting at one end of the long dining table, which was groaning under the weight of tempting cakes and neatly cut sandwiches.

"This looks great!" said Mandy, sliding onto a chair next to her dad. James took a seat beside her and started helping himself to a piece of thickly iced chocolate cake.

"So, what do you think of your rooms?" asked Dr. Adam with a smile.

"They're amazing!" Mandy replied. "Really old-fashioned, and I've even got a four-poster bed. By the way, Dad, I don't suppose you saw a cat in the hallway when you were coming down?"

Dr. Adam looked surprised. "No, I didn't." He turned to their host. "Mrs. Hapgood, does the castle have a cat?"

For the briefest of moments, Mrs. Hapgood froze. Then she smiled. "A cat?" she said. "Goodness, no! There certainly aren't any cats at Wardour."

"But we saw one," Mandy protested.

"That's simply not possible," said Mrs. Hapgood firmly, her smile fixed on her face. "There are definitely no cats here," she repeated.

Mandy felt puzzled. *What a weird reaction*, she thought. *Especially since there are so many statues of cats and so many things with cats on them wherever you look in this place.*

"That was a little strange," James whispered, echoing Mandy's thoughts.

"It was, wasn't it? Maybe the cat's a stray and Mrs. Hapgood hasn't seen it yet," she suggested.

"Maybe," James said. "But she's bound to spot it soon if it's decided to make Wardour its home. Could you pass me the orange juice, please?"

As Mandy reached for the pitcher of juice, there was a sudden commotion at the door. To her delight, Mandy saw a young beagle come bursting in. Behind him charged a young woman with a very red face. "Wait, Archie!" she called out breathlessly.

The woman was followed by a young man calling firmly, "Here, boy. Biscuit!"

At the word "biscuit," the beagle stopped in his tracks. The man quickly grabbed hold of his collar. He looked up at the guests and grinned. "He's a handful, I'm afraid! He has a mind of his own!"

"Isn't he adorable!" said Mandy, rushing over to pet the puppy, who was standing in the middle of the carpet with his tongue hanging out.

Mrs. Hapgood stared at them, looking aghast. But she quickly composed herself and in a controlled, polite voice said, "You must be Mr. and Mrs. Hitch." Without giving them a chance to reply, she went on. "I'm afraid there has been some misunderstanding." She looked at Archie and, even though she was smiling, she could not disguise her alarm. "We have a strict 'no animals' rule at Wardour. It's not fair to the other guests, you see."

The Hitches stared at her in dismay. "But we've come all the way from Kent," said Mrs. Hitch. "What are we going to do? We can't simply turn around and drive home."

"It's no problem — there's a boarding kennel in town," Mrs. Hapgood said smoothly. "It's a first-class establishment, so your dog should be perfectly all right there."

The young couple looked at each other anxiously. "I don't like the idea of leaving him there," Mrs. Hitch said to her husband, "but I don't suppose we have much choice."

"Well, let's go and inspect the place before we make a decision," said Mr. Hitch. He picked up the wriggling beagle. Mandy felt very sorry for them. How could anyone refuse to let such a cute puppy stay?

"It's not very far and Fellows will explain how to get there," Mrs. Hapgood called out as the Hitches left the room. She sighed loudly. "Most unfortunate," she said, turning back to the rest of the guests. "But let's not dwell on it. It's time to begin the weekend's mystery. I hope that most of you have had a chance to read the information packs in your rooms. If you have, you will know that we have a costume room where you can select what you would like to wear for dinner."

The guests nodded and Mrs. Hapgood went on. "The plot involves the theft of a priceless solid gold candelabra from the dining room. We know that it was taken by a member of the household. Your task is to discover who stole it and where it has been hidden. You may, of course, search the grounds and the common rooms, as well as interview the staff."

While Mrs. Hapgood was explaining the weekend's activities, Mandy found herself daydreaming, thinking about the little ginger cat. She really hoped she'd see it again. An animal-free weekend wasn't exactly Mandy's idea of fun. It would be nice to know that there weren't just pictures and statues of cats at Wardour. *After all,* Mandy told herself, *a castle wouldn't be complete without a real cat.*

Two

"I don't know how anyone could have worn clothes like these," Mandy muttered as she stared at her reflection in the mirror. She pulled at the high collar of her stiff white blouse. "I can hardly breathe in this thing." It was later that day, and she and James had gone to the costume room to choose their outfits. Now they were ready for dinner.

"Well, at least you don't look like an extra in *Oliver Twist*," said James with a grin. "How do you think I feel in this?"

Mandy turned around and immediately burst out laughing. James was wearing a baggy white shirt and a pair of brown short pants, called knickerbockers, which were tucked into thick woolen kneesocks. On his feet were a pair of pointed black shoes. "You look so funny," she said between giggles.

"Thanks!" James retorted with friendly sarcasm. "Now I feel really good about appearing in front of all the others at dinner."

"I bet they'll look pretty silly, too," Mandy reassured him as they went out into the hall. "Oops," she said, tripping over the long, tubular skirt that had wrapped itself around her ankles. She regained her balance and lifted the skirt up to her knees. "At least you can move easily in your outfit!" She sighed.

They joined the other guests in the dining room. Mandy was very impressed with her dad's outfit. Dr. Adam was wearing a brown coat with a matching short cape, and a tweed hat known as a deerstalker.

"You look like Sherlock Holmes, Dr. Adam," said James as they took their seats at the table.

"You're right, James." Dr. Adam laughed as he removed his hat. "And I intend to be as good a detective as he was. I'll be the first to sniff out the thief."

"Sounds more like a sniffing dog than a detective to me," Mandy teased.

Mentioning a dog made Mandy think about the Hitches. She realized that they weren't among the guests in the room and guessed that they had decided not to come back to Wardour.

"I see you've all managed to find suitable garments," said Mrs. Hapgood, coming in and beaming at everyone.

She, too, was dressed up for dinner in a magnificent crinoline dress and, as she moved, her long black skirt rustled noisily. "You all look wonderful — as if you'd stepped straight out of the Edwardian period!"

"And you look very elegant yourself," said one of the guests cheerfully. "I'm Geoff Russell, by the way," he added, nodding to everyone.

Mrs. Hapgood smiled at the compliment. "Dinner will be served shortly," she announced.

A thud in the wall behind Mandy and James made them spin around.

"Ah! It sounds like dinner is here already," said Mrs. Hapgood. She signaled to Fellows, who went over to the wall and slid the dark, polished panels to one side, revealing an empty compartment.

"Dinner is served in there?" James frowned.

Suddenly, several covered dishes appeared in the compartment, which was raised by unseen pulleys that creaked and grumbled behind the paneled wall.

"It's a dumbwaiter, silly." Mandy grinned. "The kitchen must be below us."

Fellows began to transfer the dishes to the table and
soon afterward, a short, cheerful-looking woman and a
red-haired girl of about eight came into the dining room.

Mrs. Hapgood stood up. "May I introduce you to our
wonderful cook," she announced. "Rebecca Moore, and
her daughter, Joanne. Mrs. Moore's family has worked
here for several generations," Mrs. Hapgood explained
proudly as the cook busied herself with the remaining
dishes. "Her great-aunt, Mary, was the first in her family
to come to Wardour."

Mrs. Moore smiled warmly at everyone, then lifted the

lid off a big silver soup tureen. A delicious smell rose into the air.

"Mmm! French onion soup," said Dr. Adam appreciatively. "My favorite!"

"All food's your favorite, Dad," Mandy teased.

"That's just the kind of guest we like here," said Mrs. Moore, putting a bowl of the steaming soup in front of Mandy. "Good, hearty eaters!"

"You've got at least two of those this time," Dr. Emily laughed, looking at her husband and James.

Joanne helped her mother and Fellows serve the soup, then came to sit next to Mandy and James.

"It must be really cool living in a castle," James said to her.

"It's great," said Joanne shyly.

Mandy picked up the linen napkin from her side plate and noticed for the first time the design in the center of the plate. A handsome ginger cat with bright green eyes gazed out from the plain white background.

Mandy laughed. "I might have guessed the dishes would be covered in cats, too," she said. "What is it with the cat theme here?"

Joanne traced the outline of the cat on her plate with her finger. "It's a shame it's just a pattern," she said. "I wish I could have my own cat."

"But we saw a ginger cat in Mandy's room earlier today!" said James quickly. "Couldn't you get to know that one?"

Joanne's eyes widened in alarm and she shot James a warning glance. "Shh," she whispered. "Mrs. Hapgood mustn't hear about it. She'll send it away."

"So you've seen it, too?" Mandy raised her eyebrows. "When we told Mrs. Hapgood about it, she didn't believe us."

"Well, Mrs. Hapgood doesn't want real cats in her perfect hotel," said Joanne. She shrugged her shoulders as if that was the end of the matter.

Fellows and Mrs. Moore cleared away the soup dishes and sent them back to the kitchen in the dumbwaiter. Shortly afterward, the dumbwaiter returned with yet more covered dishes.

Mandy eagerly accepted a bowl of vegetable lasagna, but then she wondered if she should have asked for some of the roast beef as well, even though she was a vegetarian. She could have hidden the meat in her napkin and taken it back to her room. If there was a cat hiding there, that would bring it out! *I'll just have to sneak something out at breakfast*, she thought to herself. *There's bound to be bacon and sausages on the menu.*

By the time dinner was over and coffee had been served in an adjoining lounge, it was very late and the guests began to retire to their rooms.

"We've had a long drive to get here today," said Mr. Russell, stifling a yawn. "Must get a good rest so that the brain's in good shape for tomorrow."

There were calls of "Good night" as people filtered out of the lounge and headed upstairs to the guest wing. Then there came the sound of closing doors. Mandy and James made their way up the stairs with Mandy's parents.

"'Night, Mom, 'night Dad," said Mandy.

Dr. Emily and Dr. Adam said good night and closed the door of their room behind them. Mandy and James were the only ones left in the hallway.

There were no lights at the far end of the hall, so that by the time they reached their rooms, they were shrouded in shadows. Mandy pushed open the door and quickly switched on the light. She half expected to catch a glimpse of the ginger cat again, but nothing stirred.

"Will I be glad to get out of this heavy skirt!" she said. She flopped down onto a chair and kicked off her shoes.

"And I can't wait to put on something normal — like my pajamas," said James, going over to the door that led to his room. He turned the brass knob and looked over his shoulder. "I'll wake you up in the morning," he said to Mandy.

"Oh, yes? Like you always do?" Mandy laughed, since she was usually up long before James.

"One day I might just surprise you and be the first one up," James remarked.

"I won't hold my breath waiting," Mandy called as James shut the door behind him.

Heaving a sigh of relief, she stepped out of the cumbersome Edwardian outfit and got into her pajamas. She climbed into the huge four-poster bed and closed her eyes. She expected to fall asleep right away, but instead her mind raced over the events of the day.

Somewhere in the depths of the great house, a clock started to strike. Mandy counted the echoing chimes. "Ten . . . eleven . . . twelve." And then there was silence.

Mandy shivered and pulled the covers around her. Despite the thick feather comforter, she felt cold. Suddenly, a trickle of fear ran down her spine. Somehow, she felt she wasn't alone. . . .

Mandy held her breath and strained to listen. But there wasn't a sound in the room. Slowly, she opened her eyes and, without moving her head, looked around. Pale moonlight streamed through a crack in the curtains, filling the room with a misty silver light. In the soft glow, she could see that there was nothing there —

not even a shadow on the wall. *It's only my imagination*, she tried to convince herself.

She felt a strong urge to sit up. Unable to resist, she pushed herself up onto her elbows and then, as if by a magnet, found her eyes being drawn to the door.

And there, in a pool of moonlight, sat a small ginger cat, staring back at her with enormous green eyes.

Three

"I *knew* I saw you earlier," said Mandy softly. She switched on her bedside lamp and climbed out of bed. "You must have been hiding in here all along." She frowned and looked around. "But where? We looked all over for you."

The cat stood on its hind legs and scratched at the door.

"Do you want to go out?" asked Mandy, going over to it. "I bet you do after being shut in here all this time." She bent down to stroke the pretty little animal, admiring the broad, dark ginger stripes that ran across a background of lighter ginger fur. Hastily, it shrank back out of her reach. "You're very shy," whispered Mandy. "Is that why you sneaked away from us before?"

She stood up. "All right. I won't touch you. I'll let you go," she said, opening the door just wide enough to let the cat out. "Maybe you'll be friendlier when you're used to me," she added as it slipped through the opening.

Expecting the cat to dash off instantly, Mandy put her head around the door to watch it go. But, to her surprise, it sat in the dark hallway, watching her. In the faint light seeping out from the bedroom, its beautiful green eyes glowed like emeralds.

"I thought you were desperate to get out," Mandy said.

The cat didn't move. Instead, it just sat there, gazing steadily back at her.

"Don't worry," Mandy said with a grin. "Mrs. Hapgood's in bed. She won't see you."

Still the cat didn't move. Puzzled, Mandy decided that the best solution would be to leave the door ajar. She turned to go back into bed, but something made her stop. She had the strangest feeling that the cat was trying to tell her something.

"What do you want?" she asked, looking out into the hallway again.

The cat stood up and trotted down the hall a few paces, all the while looking back at Mandy over its shoulder.

"I think I understand," said Mandy slowly. "You want me to follow you, don't you?"

The cat blinked at her, then silently padded forward a few more paces.

"Maybe you want me to open a door or a window to let you out," Mandy suggested. "Hold on a minute. I'll get my bathrobe."

She pulled on her robe then set off after the cat, which trotted down the hallway as soon as Mandy came out the door. "Not so fast," Mandy whispered, breaking into a run to keep up.

But the cat ran faster still, its paws skimming the carpet. *It looks like it's not even touching the ground*, Mandy thought. At the same time, she hoped that the sound of her own footsteps pounding rapidly over the carpet wouldn't wake anyone — especially Mrs. Hapgood.

Ahead of Mandy, the cat's ginger coat and the sparkling green flash of its eyes gleamed in the shadows cast by the dim lights. Mandy's own dark shadow kept pace with her, flickering over the carpet at her feet.

The cat paused at the top of the stairs, swishing its tail from side to side. Then it gave Mandy a look of such longing it took her breath away.

"What is it, little one?" Mandy asked in a hushed, gentle voice.

The cat seemed to nod, as if reassured that Mandy

was still following, then continued silently on its way, gliding down the main staircase to the entrance hall.

Mandy followed, and when she'd reached the bottom of the stairs, the cat went on, vanishing down a narrower staircase opposite Mrs. Hapgood's office.

Mandy hurried across the empty, echoing space, the cold of the tiles seeping into her bare feet. Moonlight filtered into the hall through the tall windows on either side of the entrance door, filling the stairwell with gray and silver shadows.

I think it's going to the kitchen, reasoned Mandy. *Perhaps it wants me to let it out into the courtyard.* She ran down the stairs, just in time to see the cat dash into a doorway. Mandy was about to go through the door when a faint whispering sound swam out into the bare, stone hallway. Someone was talking softly in the room beyond.

"There you are, Puss," came the hushed voice. "Where have you been?"

Mandy stopped and listened.

"Here's your food, my girl," said the mysterious voice. It sounded like a young boy.

Mandy tiptoed through the doorway and found herself in the long basement kitchen. A boy of about twelve stood in a soft pool of light in the middle of the room, surrounded by half a dozen cats twining themselves fondly around his legs, opening their mouths wide in hushed meows.

The boy was dressed in old-fashioned clothes, very much like the outfit James had worn to dinner. The cats watched him closely, their tails flicking in anticipation, as he put bowls of food on the floor. As he bent down, his thick red hair flopped forward, concealing his face.

He was so absorbed in the cats that he seemed completely unaware of Mandy's presence. The cat from Mandy's room twirled and twisted lovingly around his legs. The boy stroked her, whispering affectionately, "Puss, Puss, where have you been today?"

Then he picked up two tabby kittens. "There, my precious ones," he crooned. "Aren't you growing into strong boys?" In an admiring tone he added, "You're going to be the pride of the castle, all right."

The pride of the castle! Mandy felt very confused. *What was he talking about? Cats were banned from Wardour!*

Mandy wondered who the boy was. He wasn't one of the guests. Was he one of the kitchen staff? *His voice is so strange*, she thought to herself. *It sounds as if he were in an echo chamber.*

She took a few steps forward. The boy looked up at her.

Mandy's heart skipped a beat. She was looking at a

face that was so pale it was almost translucent. "Who are you?" she asked hoarsely, taking a step back.

The boy said nothing, but continued to stare across the room with a serious expression. Mandy was reminded of the way Puss had looked at her so earnestly on the landing.

"You're up late. Is there anything I can do to help?" Mandy persisted. As she waited for his reply, she stepped forward, but in the poor light she didn't notice the empty cart on wheels just in front of her. She bumped into it, sending it clattering across the floor.

"Oh, no!" Mandy muttered guiltily. "This will wake the whole castle." The cart crashed noisily into the big stove at the far wall and bounced back, tipping noisily onto its side. "Eh, that's it!"

She turned back to the boy and gasped in surprise. He was no longer there! And neither were the cats. Slowly, Mandy began to back out of the room. Before she had a chance to turn around, a harsh light lit up the kitchen, dazzling her. She blinked in the strong glare, trying to make sense of what was happening.

And then a deep voice rang out from behind her, "What are you doing here?"

FELES DEFENSOR

Four

Mandy spun around to see the butler standing behind her. "Fellows!" she cried. "You made me jump!" Letting out a long breath, she felt her heartbeat return to normal.

"I'm sorry," he said. "I didn't mean to alarm you, but I heard a noise and came to investigate."

"And I'm sorry I disturbed you," Mandy apologized. "I bumped into a rolling cart by mistake."

"Mmm, I see," murmured the man. "But what were you doing in the kitchen? It's the middle of the night!"

Mandy hesitated. She wasn't sure how to explain about the cat leading her to the kitchen. If there were meant to be no cats at Wardour, would Fellows believe her?

"Were you hungry?" the butler prompted.

"Not at all," said Mandy. She took a deep breath. She might as well tell the truth — even if he didn't take her seriously. "You see, I was following a cat and —"

"Impossible," Fellows interrupted.

"What?" asked Mandy, surprised by such a strong reaction even before she'd finished her story.

"You could not have been following a cat. There aren't any here," Fellows said emphatically. He put a hand on her shoulder and started to guide her through the door. "Now you must go back to bed."

Mandy shrugged off his hand and turned around. She stared at the room which, only a minute or so before, had been full of contented cats. Now, not a trace of them was left — not even a bowl or a scrap of food. "I definitely saw one . . . lots of them," she insisted.

Fellows gave a sharp cough. "Nonsense," he said, his voice pitched higher than before. "You were probably — er — sleepwalking and woke up when you bumped into the cart."

Mandy shook her head. "I was wide awake. And I wasn't the only one," she said. Then, watching Fellows closely, she added, "There was a boy in here, too."

To Mandy's surprise, he didn't laugh. Instead, a look of anxiety flitted across the butler's face. His eyes darted from side to side as he quickly glanced around the kitchen. Then he looked back down at her and cleared his throat. "It must have been a dream," he said firmly. "Everyone is asleep. Now, you really must go back to bed."

"But —" Mandy began to protest but Fellows would not allow her to go on. He stepped to one side and again guided her gently through the door.

Mandy realized there was no point in arguing with him. He would not hear her out. In fact, almost without her being aware of it, he had quietly closed the door behind her and she was now alone on the drafty stairs leading up to the entrance hall.

"Oh, well." Mandy sighed. She was about to leave when she thought she heard the butler's voice again. She paused and listened. Quite distinctly, she could hear the old man murmuring. "That's all we need," she heard him say. Then his voice trailed off and Mandy was left wondering what he meant.

Mandy realized that she was shivering. But this time it really was because of the cold. The chill from the stone steps had spread right up through her. A warm bed seemed like a very good idea. She took a step forward but stopped immediately. In the kitchen, Fellows was speaking again. "You should be careful who sees you, Joe," he said softly. "Not everyone will keep your secret safe."

Mandy felt stunned. So Fellows knew about the boy in the kitchen, after all! And his name was Joe. *But who is he?* she asked herself. *And why does Fellows have to keep him a secret?*

A tiny creaking noise warned Mandy that Fellows was opening the kitchen door. She whirled around and dashed back up to the entrance hall, then up the staircase to the gallery before he could catch her eavesdropping. She peered down just in time to see the long, narrow shadow of the butler moving across the entrance hall and disappearing toward the other end of the castle.

Mandy yawned and realized that she was exhausted. She hurried back to her bedroom and climbed gratefully into the soft bed. She would work out just what she had seen in the morning.

"Wake up, Mandy. We'll be late for breakfast." James's voice sounded in Mandy's head, bringing her out of a deep sleep.

She struggled to open her eyes.

"Come on, Mandy. It's already eight-thirty," James urged. "We have to be at breakfast in time to find out the next clue to the mystery, remember?"

Mystery! Mandy remembered the mystery, all right. Only it wasn't the stolen candelabra she was thinking about. The memory of the strange events in the night propelled her into action. She sat up quickly, rubbing her eyes.

James, dressed once more in the comical knicker-bockers, was grinning at her. "Didn't I tell you I'd surprise you one day and be the first one up?" he said.

Mandy pushed a strand of hair out of her face. "Uh-huh. But I have an even bigger surprise for you," she told him. "Listen to this." She described what she'd seen during the night — the timid ginger cat that led her down to the kitchen, the boy feeding a whole crowd of cats, and the way they had disappeared when the cart banged into the stove . . .

James's eyes were wide with wonder as Mandy came to the end of the story. "That's incredible!" he exclaimed, pushing his glasses up the bridge of his nose. "I wish I'd been there, too."

"So do I," said Mandy. "I would have woken you if I'd known what was going to happen." She looked seriously at James. "You know, I've been thinking about it. The way those cats disappeared, the fact that Puss didn't make any noise, the way that boy looked . . . James, I think I might have seen some ghosts."

James's eyebrows shot up into his hair. Then he nodded slowly. "You could be right. Tell you what, why don't we talk to Joanne at breakfast, to find out if she's seen anything?"

"Good idea," said Mandy. "Come on, let's get going."

She jumped out of bed and hurried into the bathroom to wash and dress. The cumbersome Edwardian skirt hardly bothered her now that she had so much else on her mind.

As they entered the dining room, Mandy was pleased to see that Joanne was there. She sat down next to her and said quietly, "I saw that ginger cat again last night."

"Did you?" replied Joanne, looking excited. "Where?"

"In my room and later in the kitchen," Mandy told her. "Have you ever seen any other cats in there?"

"Well . . . ," Joanne began, just as Mrs. Hapgood came into the dining room.

"Good morning, everyone," said the hotel owner, smiling graciously at her guests. "I hope you all slept well."

There were nods of agreement all around except from Mandy, who leaned over to James. "At least *she* didn't hear me creeping around in the night," she whispered.

Mrs. Hapgood was handing out pieces of paper that

held the next clue to the mystery game. "Perhaps you three would like to work together," she suggested when she came to Mandy, James, and Joanne. She gave them their sheet of paper. "You might even be better at unraveling the mystery than the adults!" she added.

James grinned. "We will be," he told her confidently.

Mrs. Hapgood raised her eyebrows slightly. "Well, good luck!" She smiled.

As the woman walked away from them, Mandy turned to Joanne again. "You were going to tell us if you'd seen any other cats," she reminded her.

Keeping an eye on Mrs. Hapgood in case she turned back, Joanne said shyly, "Yes, I have seen some — in the kitchen. Only . . . ," she hesitated.

"Only what?" Mandy pressed her gently.

"Only — they always just — er — *vanished* — the minute I spotted them," Joanne explained. Under her breath, she added, "It's almost as if they aren't *real* cats at all."

"I've seen them, too," Mandy said quietly. She glanced at James, who nodded encouragingly. "And if there really aren't any live cats here at Wardour, like Mrs. Hapgood says, then we think they must be *ghosts* of cats. Do you know if anyone else has seen them?"

Joanne stared at her, dumbfounded. "I don't think so," she managed to say at last.

"I think we can be pretty sure Mrs. Hapgood hasn't seen them," said James practically. "Living animals are bad enough, but," he said and then chuckled softly, "ghostly ones would probably make her close the hotel instantly!"

"Yes, but remember how touchy she was yesterday when I told her about the cat we saw in my room," said Mandy. "Maybe she *has* seen something odd and she's worried the guests will find out."

Mrs. Hapgood interrupted their hushed conversation by passing around a neatly typed list of places of interest close to Wardour Castle. "When you're not too busy solving the mystery, you might like to explore some of these," she suggested brightly. "There's a well-stocked museum in the town," she told them. "It has a painting of Wardour Castle in it dating from the sixteenth century."

But Mandy wasn't interested in the local tourist attractions. She was anxious to start looking for more information about the castle's cat history. She hastily finished her toast and folded up her napkin.

Just as she stood up, she heard a strange noise. A shrill and plaintive howl was coming from somewhere in the room. Mandy looked around, expecting the others to have heard it. But everyone, including James, seemed deaf to it. Mandy stood stock-still, feeling her skin crawl as the eerie feline wailing echoed around her. It was as if she alone were hearing a cat calling dismally from another time.

She shook her head as the melancholy sound surged and fell, then finally faded away. Mandy became aware once more of the voices of the guests and the sounds of breakfast being eaten, but she could not shake off the feelings of loss and urgency that the wailing had suggested to her. Mandy knew instinctively that this was another summons to help the cats, just as Puss had shown her the ghostly scene in the kitchen the night before.

A voice broke into her thoughts. "We're off to explore the herb garden, Mandy," Dr. Emily was saying. "And then we might go into town for coffee. What about you three? Where do your clues lead you?"

"We're not sure yet," said Mandy. "We still have to work them out."

"Ah. Confusion already!" Dr. Adam laughed. "What you need is a Sherlock Holmes on your team." With a flourish of his cloak he swaggered over to the door. "See you at lunchtime!" he called behind him.

Before Mandy, James, and Joanne could leave, Fellows came in. "Good morning. Did you all sleep well?" he asked, looking pointedly at Mandy. He picked up a silver goblet from the oak sideboard and began to polish it.

"Not really," replied Mandy, returning his direct gaze.

She noticed that the goblet was engraved with the same elegant cat that appeared on the side plates. It was slender and poised, and its huge almond-shaped eyes looked very familiar. Mandy took a deep breath. She was sure she had heard Fellows talking to the boy — Joe — last night. That meant he had to have seen the cats, too. Here was her chance to find out what he knew.

"That's a beautiful cat on there," Mandy said, trying to sound casual. She watched the butler closely.

"Mmm," murmured Fellows as if completely absorbed in his task. He put down the first goblet and started on the next.

James seemed to guess what Mandy was doing. "Is it an engraving of a special cat?" he asked.

Fellows shook his head and continued polishing, but Mandy was sure he had hesitated for the briefest of moments. She decided to come straight to the point. "This place is full of cats," she declared.

Fellows paused and stared at the yellow polishing cloth in his hand. Then, in a measured tone, he said, "Indeed. And as young Joanne here could have pointed out to you, there is a cat motif throughout the castle."

"Is there a reason for that?" Mandy asked politely. "I've never seen anything like it before. This place must have an amazing history of cat lovers!"

Fellows put down the goblet and ran a hand over his balding head. He glanced at the door as if to make sure no one were around. Then, in a low voice, he began. "Probably the single most important thing about Wardour," he said, "was the colony of cats that lived here for as long as anyone could remember. They were so important that a kitchen boy was always employed to feed them and look after them."

Mandy was startled, but there was no time to ask any questions because Fellows was continuing with his story.

"The owners of the castle adored the cats because they did a wonderful job of keeping down the mouse population. Neighboring farms were almost overrun at times, but not Wardour."

"And so the owners decorated the castle with cats, in honor of them?" offered James.

"That's right," said Fellows. "Have a look at this." He beckoned them over to the far end of the room and pointed to a richly colored tapestry hanging on the wall. Into it was woven an elaborate coat-of-arms featuring two ginger cats, and underneath was a motto: FELES DE-FENSOR.

"Feelies defensor," Joanne read out loud.

Fellows chuckled. "Actually, it's pronounced *feelays,*" he said. "It's Latin for *'The cat is my protector.'* Well, more or less!" He glanced back at the door again, then, in a very low voice, added, "You probably won't be sur-prised to learn that Wardour is not the original name for the castle. It was once known as Castle Feles."

Far from clearing up things in Mandy's mind, this in-formation made her more puzzled than ever. "But if the cats were so important that the castle was even named after them, why has it all changed?" she asked.

Fellows seemed reluctant to continue talking to them. He went back over to the sideboard and picked up another goblet.

"Who changed the name?" Mandy persisted, follow-ing him across the thick carpet.

Fellows concentrated on the goblet for a few moments. Then he sighed and put it back on the sideboard. He turned to face them, and in a hushed voice he related the rest of the story. "Mrs. Hapgood," he said, in answer to Mandy's question. "She banished all the cats and changed the name when she inherited the castle from a distant relative a few years ago. I think she was worried that people wouldn't come here if there were cats all over the place." He flicked an invisible speck of dust off his sleeve. "After all, she had to make a success of the business to make sure Wardour survived. Stately homes are very expensive to maintain."

"It's a shame it was at the cats' expense, though," said Mandy. "Especially since they were here first."

"I agree," said the butler sympathetically.

Mandy was surprised. She hadn't for a minute thought that Fellows might have been on the cats' side. After all, Mrs. Hapgood was his employer.

"After changing the name of the castle, she started to remove as much evidence of the cats as she could," Fellows went on.

"Is that why she redecorated the bedrooms?" asked James.

Fellows nodded. "Partly," he said. "But she was mainly concerned with making the suites more comfortable for

her guests. Not everyone would appreciate a cat theme!"
He smiled wryly at them.

"But it's what makes the castle different!" Mandy
cried out. "They're part of its heritage. Mrs. Hapgood
must understand that!" She felt a stab of anxiety. If Mrs.
Hapgood continued to remove all the cat-themed decorations, very soon all traces of the castle's history would
be gone forever.

"What about the biggest cat items?" she asked, hopefully. "Like the statues in the hall and," she pointed to
the coat-of-arms on the wall, "the tapestries? She hasn't
got plans to get rid of those, has she?"

"Some things she won't touch," explained Fellows.
"They're too valuable, and the tapestry in particular is a
very rare example from the sixteenth century."

"And she'll never be able to get rid of the mystery
cats," announced Joanne cheerfully.

Fellows looked startled. "Mystery cats, Joanne? What
are you talking about?" he asked, sounding uncomfortable. "You know there's no such thing here." Then, before Joanne could reply, he looked at Mandy and said,
"You'd be interested to know that somewhere in the
castle are some very old documents that record the
history of the cats and the dreadful plagues of mice.
They show quite clearly how important the cats were in

fighting off the rats and mice and protecting the harvest."

"Didn't Mrs. Hapgood know about those records?" asked James. "She might not have gotten rid of the cats, then."

Fellows glanced quickly toward the door. "She never knew about them," he explained. "A long time ago, they were taken from their cabinet here in the dining room and hidden."

"Who hid them?" asked Mandy. "And where?"

"Old castles like this often have secret rooms —" began the butler, but the sound of footsteps outside interrupted him. Swiftly, he straightened up and turned his back on the children. No sooner had he picked up another goblet and begun to polish it, than Mrs. Hapgood entered.

"Still here, you three?" she asked, her eyebrows arched in surprise.

"We were — er — trying to get Fellows to give us some more clues," Mandy said quickly.

"I'm afraid you're asking the wrong person for information," Mrs. Hapgood said. "If anyone can keep things to himself, it's Fellows." She smiled confidently.

Mandy smiled, too. If only Mrs. Hapgood knew what the butler had just been telling them!

As Mrs. Hapgood started to give Fellows more instructions about cleaning the silver, Mandy decided it was a good time to start exploring the rest of the castle. She led the way back to their rooms to change into their ordinary clothes, her mind full of what they'd just learned. "If only we could find those documents," she told James earnestly.

"I know," he answered. "I bet a lot of guests would be really interested to learn about the true history of this castle."

"And if that meant more people came to stay here," said Mandy, "Mrs. Hapgood might see just how important the cats are." She stopped by the window on the landing and traced a finger around the pattern of a cat on the curtain. "She might even be persuaded to let them come back to Wardour for good."

Five

"Where should we start?" Mandy asked when the three of them met up again fifteen minutes later, after changing out of their costumes. They were in the gallery above the entrance hall and, instead of pursuing the weekend mystery, they were determined to find the hidden documents that Fellows had described to them. With a shiver, Mandy recalled the wailing she had heard. She was sure now that the ghost cats had been appealing to her to uncover the castle's secret cat history.

"How about the garden?" suggested James.

"The garden!" Mandy exclaimed. "I don't think we'll find any secret rooms out there."

"I know," said James. "But we will be able to count all the windows."

"How will that help?" Joanne asked doubtfully.

"Because if there are more windows than rooms, we should be able to figure out if there are any hidden chambers," James explained.

They ran down the stairs and were halfway across the hall when Mrs. Hapgood suddenly appeared from her office. "Onto something promising?" she asked, her arms folded in front of her and her head to one side.

"You bet!" said James. He waved his sheet of clues confidently.

"How interesting," said Mrs. Hapgood with a smile. "I hope you're on the right track."

"We're just checking something outdoors to make sure we're right," Mandy replied.

"Careful," whispered James once they were out of earshot in the parking area. "Don't let on too much."

"I won't," Mandy reassured him. "But at least every-one else is also hunting around, so it will look like we're doing the same thing."

"Good point," said James. "So we'll tell everyone ex-actly what we're doing and they'll think we're talking about the stolen candelabra, when really we mean the historical papers."

They ran across the wide lawn until they had a good

view of the front of the castle. James pulled a notebook and pencil out of his pocket and made a quick sketch of the three-storied building, filling in the windows as Mandy and Joanne counted them.

Once they'd finished with the front, they went to each side and made a note of the windows there before going around to the back.

They counted the rear windows, double-checking to make sure they hadn't missed any in the numerous nooks and crannies. With their heads spinning with numbers, they went to sit in an open-fronted summerhouse, which faced a sunken rose garden.

"Sixty-one," said James, adding up the total. "Now we need to find out which rooms have more than one window so that we can work out exactly how many rooms there are."

"That means we're going to have to go through the *entire* castle," said Mandy. "The guest rooms, staff quarters — everywhere. I don't know if we'll be able to do that."

"Mmm. You've got a point there," said James, staring across the rose garden. "There must be some other way of finding out."

"There is!" Joanne exclaimed, jumping out of the swinging bench they were sitting in. Her sudden leap rocked the seat violently.

"Uh-oh," grunted James, grabbing hold of one of the side supports. But as he leaned over, his weight caused the suspended bench to lurch even farther, and he was tipped out onto the rough ground.

"Sorry, James!" cried Joanne, kneeling down next to him. "I shouldn't have jumped out like that. I just remembered that there's an old map of the castle in the library. It shows you where all the rooms are on each floor. I should have thought of it before."

"That sounds like exactly what we need," said James, cramming the notebook back into his pocket. "So what are we waiting for? Let's go!" he called, starting back the way they had come.

"Wait!" Joanne shouted after him. "We don't have to go all the way around to the front again. We can go in the back way, through the kitchen. Follow me."

She led them through the rose garden and past a walled vegetable garden where a cheerful young gardener lifted his cap to them.

"Found anything yet?" he called.

"No. But we're definitely onto something," replied James.

"Are you?" The gardener grinned. "I'll be interested to hear what you find." Then he dug his spade into the soil again, laughing softly.

As they wound their way between the beds of leeks

and peas, Mandy heard the gardener's laughter dying down behind them. Just when it faded completely, another wave of chuckling broke out. It sounded much younger somehow, like a boy's. She spun around to see what was making the gardener laugh now, but he was bent over his digging, grunting with the effort of lifting the damp soil.

"Can you two hear that?" she asked James and Joanne.

"Hear what?" asked James.

"That laughing," said Mandy. She could still hear it bouncing off the redbrick wall of the vegetable garden and ringing out around her. A tingling shiver ran through Mandy. The laughter sounded happy and unthreatening, but where was it coming from?

"It was just the gardener," said James.

Joanne led them across a walled courtyard, then through a wooden door into a damp, cool scullery. The tiled floor was worn and shiny from the hundreds of feet that had walked upon it over the years, and an enormous stone sink stood against one wall, rubbed smooth from centuries of use. A massive fireplace built into another wall housed a heavy-looking iron pot, blackened from all the fires that had blazed around it.

Mandy tried to picture all the hard work that had taken place there. Red-faced servants would have been stoking up the fire to boil water in the pot. Others would have carried the boiling water over to the sink to wash piles of dirty dishes brought down from the banquets upstairs. Scullery maids and kitchen boys would have been scrubbing the floors and emptying out the buckets of dirty water.

I'm glad I was born in this age, Mandy thought, noticing the one modern item in the scullery — a big automatic dishwasher. As she stared at the machine, a fleeting shadow behind it caught her eye.

"A cat!" she whispered to herself as a hint of orange flashed out of sight. Mandy turned to James and Joanne. "I'm sure I've just seen a ginger cat chasing something behind the dishwasher," she told them, pointing excitedly.

"Did you really?" said Joanne, looking hopefully toward the machine.

"Yes," said Mandy. She stepped forward and, placing her head against the smooth stone wall, she peered behind the dishwasher. She just caught a glimpse of a long, thin body whisking out of sight. Definitely a cat — and not just any cat. Mandy was sure it had been Puss — this cat had the same distinctive light and dark ginger stripes.

Mandy was just about to call James and Joanne over, when the sound of voices in the kitchen interrupted them. "I saw a couple in the scullery just this morning. They ran behind the dishwasher," said a woman. It sounded like Joanne's mother.

"But we've never had mice before!" exclaimed the other voice, sounding horrified.

"Oops! That's my mom and Mrs. Hapgood," said Joanne. "I'm not really allowed to bring anyone in here."

"We'll say we're following up a clue," said James quickly.

Joanne grinned at him. "Good idea," she said. "My mom can't argue with that!"

At that moment, Mrs. Hapgood burst into the scullery, closely followed by Mrs. Moore, who was looking rather breathless and red in the face.

"Oh!" said Mrs. Hapgood, stopping abruptly. "What are you doing here, children?"

"Just passing through on our way to find something out," said James cheerfully. He pretended to check one of the clues on his sheet of paper. Then he turned to Mandy and Joanne and nodded confidently. "Yup, it's definitely upstairs," he said, leading the way out of the scullery.

As she followed James and Joanne across the kitchen, Mandy heard Mrs. Hapgood talking to Mrs. Moore again. She paused and strained to listen.

"Well, if the mice become more of a problem, we'll

have to buy some traps or poison to deal with them,"
Mrs. Hapgood was saying.

Mandy felt a shiver of alarm. *Were mice returning to
Wardour Castle?* she wondered.

Mrs. Hapgood's voice faded as she and Mrs. Moore
made their way into the garden. Mandy looked around
the kitchen. How different it looked in the light of day.
The cart she had bumped into last night stood against a
whitewashed wall, laden with a tray of gleaming knives
and forks. On top of the stove, two enormous stainless-
steel pots gave off thin wisps of aromatic steam. A long,
pine table beneath the window was almost hidden under baskets of newly picked vegetables and loaves of
freshly baked bread. Mandy sniffed appreciatively.

Everything in the kitchen spoke of busy activity,
catering to a castle full of guests. It was hard even to
imagine the scene of the night before — the mysterious
boy and the group of cats milling around in the center
of the room. Had she *really* seen a room full of ghosts?

A sudden realization hit Mandy. *If the cats had been
real, then Mrs. Hapgood wouldn't have to worry about
mice in the scullery right now*, she thought. And now it
looked as if it were even more important for the cats to
come back to the castle. But they still needed to find the
secret room and the hidden documents.

Mandy hurried out of the kitchen and followed James and Joanne up the stone steps to the entrance hall.

"Which way to the library?" James asked. "I want to have a look at this floor plan."

"It's next door to the dining room," answered Joanne, beckoning them along the hallway. She pushed open a heavy pair of dark wooden doors and disappeared inside.

Mandy and James followed her and gasped when they found themselves in a large, oak-floored room that looked as if nothing had been changed in it for a hundred years.

Hundreds of books lined the walls from floor to ceiling. Mandy noticed that most of them were leather-bound, and some of the volumes looked very old indeed. She peered at the titles on the books nearest to her, but the gold lettering was too faded to read easily.

"The floor plan is over here," said Joanne, going across to a wide glass-topped desk.

Beneath the glass lay a large sheet of yellowing paper. Intricate line drawings detailed the layout of the castle, with labels written down each side in curly old-fashioned handwriting. A heading at the top boldly stated the castle's original name — CASTLE FELES.

"I always thought that meant something to do with the drawings," said Joanne, running her finger along the glass above the heading. "I didn't realize it was the name of the castle."

James winked at Joanne. "That's because you don't speak Latin." He grinned.

"I do now," Joanne responded. With mock gravity she pronounced, *"Feles defensor."*

"Very impressive," said Mandy, coming to join them at the desk.

At that moment, she heard a hushed mewing sound that grew dizzyingly loud, a chorus of purring and meowing that filled her ears. As she stared down at the map, the drawings swirled and melted before her eyes, reshaping themselves to show the face of a cat.

"Puss!" Mandy said in astonishment.

The whiskers on the little ginger face twitched and the jewellike eyes held Mandy firmly in their intense gaze. As she recognized the same desperate plea for help as before, a wave of frustration welled up inside her.

"Tell me what I must do!" she whispered urgently.

Puss blinked her eyes sadly, then opened her mouth in a heartrending meow that was instantly swallowed up in the uproar of cat voices still echoing in Mandy's ears.

Mandy sighed helplessly and, in that instant, the ginger face was gone. Mandy was looking again at the drawings.

"What are you muttering about, Mandy?" asked James,

leaning on his elbows while he squinted at her with a puzzled look on his face.

With a jolt, Mandy became aware that she was the only one who had seen the face of the mysterious cat. "Oh, just that I hope the *feles* will have another chance to *defend*," she told him, deciding not to try to explain what had just happened. But she was even more determined to help Puss now. Could this mean that they were getting close to finding the hidden documents?

Mandy stared down at the drawings, identifying the summerhouse and also a small building at the edge of the grounds that was labeled "Chapel." James and Joanne were poring over the plan that was divided into three sections, one for each floor. They were counting the windows under their breath, and jotting down numbers in James's notebook.

"So, according to this," said Joanne as she straightened up again, "there are sixty windows in the castle."

"And we counted sixty-one outside," James reminded them. "Which means there's definitely another room somewhere that isn't shown on these diagrams." He turned back a page in his notebook and tried to compare his rough sketches with the architect's original drawing. Mandy leaned over his shoulder to watch.

Matching the drawings window for window, James finally decided that the hidden chamber had to be somewhere close to the library and dining room. "It looks like I've drawn one more window here than there is on the map," he said. "But it's hard to tell because my sketches aren't very accurate."

"At least they give us a starting point," said Mandy. Then, with a grin, she added, "Of course, in all the old movies, secret rooms are always hidden behind the bookshelves in the library!"

"You know, that's not a bad idea," James remarked, going over to one of the walls. "Let's find out how much of a movie set this library is," he said. He studied the bookshelves closely and tugged experimentally at a carved wooden cat fixed to the wall beside the window.

Mandy looked at Joanne and shrugged. "It's worth a try," she said. She pointed to the wall next to the door, which was paneled in dark oak. "You try over there, Joanne," Mandy said. "That wall could be much thicker than it looks, and there might be something hidden behind it."

For the next fifteen minutes, they tapped, poked, and tugged their way around the library, looking for a hidden lever, a false book, or any other evidence of a concealed chamber. But they could find nothing out of the ordinary.

Eventually, James proposed that they try somewhere else. "This is one library that isn't true to the movies,"

he said, climbing down a stepladder after checking the topmost shelf of books.

"Let's try the dining room next," Mandy suggested, helping James fold up the ladder and lean it against the paneled wall.

"We'll have to hurry because it's nearly lunchtime," Joanne pointed out.

They ran next door into the dining room, trying to appear casual in case someone was in there. Fortunately, the room was empty.

"Quick, let's check the place out," Mandy whispered. As James and Joanne began lifting the tapestry carefully away from the wall to see if there was anything behind it, Mandy went over to the wooden panels that concealed the dumbwaiter. Since the door to the dumbwaiter was so successfully camouflaged, there could be another secret compartment close by. But the rest of the wall sounded very solid when Mandy tapped it, and none of the panels moved when she tried to slide them to one side.

She sat down thoughtfully on a low bench beneath the window. It was covered with a beautiful cushion embroidered with the familiar pattern of elegant ginger cats, twining their slender bodies through dark green leaves. Mandy absentmindedly ran her finger along a delicate strand of ivy as she tried to imagine where a builder would put a secret room.

Surely not up a sooty chimney, she thought with amusement as she watched James groping around inside the fireplace. And then she remembered reading about special "priests' holes" — cramped cubbyholes that were built up chimneys to hide priests from their enemies.

But this was one chimney that didn't have any secrets, for James backed out onto the hearth declaring with exasperation, "Not a thing." He wiped his hand across his forehead, leaving a sooty smudge above one eye.

Joanne straightened out a Persian rug she'd lifted up, and then she sighed. "The trouble is, the castle is just so *big*. It could be *anywhere*," she said.

"What could be anywhere?" The unexpected question from the door startled them all.

Mandy looked across to see Fellows entering with a tray of glasses. She relaxed. Fellows must have guessed that they would be looking for the cat documents. They had nothing to hide from him. "The secret room you told us about," she answered. "Do you know where it is?"

The butler put the tray on the table and in a low, calm voice said, "If I could tell you that, I would." Then he turned and walked out of the dining room without another word.

Mandy jumped off the window seat and ran after him. "Does that mean you can't tell us or that you don't know?" she called.

But Fellows didn't reply, and Mandy reached the door in time to see him hurrying across the hall. She watched him disappear down the kitchen stairs, then she went back into the dining room. "It looks like we'll just have to keep searching," she announced.

Six

As soon as lunch was over, Mandy, James, and Joanne continued their hunt. They started in the drawing room, on the opposite side of the hall to the dining room. Finding nothing out of the ordinary there, they went on to the entrance hall, then finally they searched the long hallways that ran the length of the castle. Even though James had seemed confident that the secret room had to be somewhere near the library and the dining room, Mandy still thought they should check the rest of the castle.

"Not a thing," said Mandy, frowning with exasperation after they'd explored the hallways on all three stories.

63

They sat at the bottom of the staircase in the entrance hall and stared across the black and white tiles. Through the long windows on either side of the front door, Mandy spotted a small herd of deer grazing peacefully on the grounds beyond the fountain. She turned to James and Joanne. "Let's go outside and watch the deer for a while," she suggested, jumping up and leading the way across the echoing hall, out into the warm sun.

The noise of the water spouting from the fountain drowned out any sound their footsteps made as they cautiously approached the deer. One young doe had wandered away from the rest of the herd, toward the castle. Standing with its back to them, and with a gentle breeze blowing their scent away from it, the shy animal was oblivious to their presence.

Mandy walked quietly over to the low wall that edged the pond and sat down. James and Joanne sat down next to her, and they watched with delight as the deer nibbled daintily at the neatly trimmed lawn just a few yards from them.

Suddenly, the peaceful scene was interrupted by the crunching sound of tires on gravel. With a jerk, the deer lifted her head. She looked around nervously as a car swooped up the drive and swung into the parking area. A door opened and then slammed shut as a guest jumped out and walked toward the front door.

With a graceful leap, the deer took off and joined the rest of the herd as they bounded away to the safety of the woods on the far side of the drive.

"Too bad," said James, standing up and stretching. "It was nice to get so close without her knowing we were here." He climbed onto the low wall and looked around. "What's this?" he asked, pointing to dense shrubbery on the other side of the parking area. "It looks like a maze."

"It is," said Joanne. She stood up and brushed off the seat of her jeans.

"Hey! That's great!" James exclaimed, jumping off the wall. "Let's check it out."

"It's really hard," Joanne warned him as they ran over to the network of hedges. "I tried it once when I was little and got totally lost."

"What happened to you?" asked Mandy.

"I screamed for help until Fellows came and showed me the way out." Joanne grinned. "I've never been in it again."

Mandy noticed a slender gray tower just visible above the hedges. "What's that?" she asked.

"Oh, that's the tower that marks the center of the maze," Joanne explained. "I never managed to get to it, though."

Suddenly, James stopped. "Look!" he exclaimed. "There's the cat again!"

A ginger cat was sitting in the sun at the entrance to the maze. It was watching them carefully, its green eyes wide and its body alert, ready to dash away in a second.

"Is that Puss?" James asked Mandy eagerly.

"I don't think so," she replied slowly. "This cat's got a white V-shape on its chest. I don't remember seeing that on Puss."

"Does that mean it's another ghost?" James asked.

"How can it be a ghost in the daytime?" said Joanne. "Ghosts aren't supposed to come out in the light, are they?"

Mandy shrugged. "Well, I'm sure I saw a cat in the scullery this morning," she said. She felt puzzled. The cat that had visited her in the night had seemed so sad and desperate, as if it were asking Mandy for her help. This cat sitting by the maze looked much more wary of the approaching humans. Its tail flicked nervously as they approached.

Mandy took a few more steps toward it, which made the cat's muscles tense further. Just then, a harsh, squeaking noise came from the gravel path that led around the side of the castle. At once, the cat spun around and hurtled through the opening to the maze, disappearing with a final flick of its striped ginger tail.

James dashed after it but stopped abruptly in the entrance and looked from side to side, trying to spot which way it had gone. Eventually, he shook his head. "Vanished!" he said. He folded his arms and sighed. "That's a pretty strange ghost, if it was scared off by a noise!" he commented. "Mandy, are you *sure* that the cat you saw last night was a ghost?"

"I think so," said Mandy, remembering the way Joe and his cats had disappeared as soon as the cart hit the stove.

The squeak grew louder and soon the cause of it became clear as the gardener appeared around the corner, pushing a metal wheelbarrow filled with dead leaves.

"Hello, again," he said with a friendly smile. He stopped and lowered the wheelbarrow, then kicked the wheel with a mud-encrusted rubber boot. "Irritating noise this thing makes," he said, bending down to fiddle with the wheel.

"Maybe it needs some oil," James suggested.

"I don't think so," said the gardener, standing up and lifting the handles again. "I tried that already. It might be a loose bearing." He stamped his feet, loosening more mud from his boots. "Trying the maze, are you?" he asked.

"Yes," said James. "If you hear us calling, you'll come and find us, won't you?" He turned to Mandy. "Do you want to lead the way?" he offered.

"Why? So you can blame me when we get lost?" she

said with a grin. She was just as eager as James was to explore the maze. At least it meant she might have another chance to see that mysterious cat. Mandy craned her head back and looked again at the gray tower looming in the center of the maze. She felt a desperate urge to get to the mysterious stone building. She took Joanne's hand and stepped through the entrance.

In silence, they followed the narrow path between the high hedges, sometimes going through a gap and other times having to turn back when they came up against a solid wall of green leaves. Even the sounds of birds faded as they ventured deeper into the shrubbery. The hedges were so tall that they completely lost sight of the tower.

"We don't even know if we're close to the center yet or still somewhere on the edge!" James broke the silence, sounding exasperated, as they turned a corner and found themselves going back in the same direction from which they had just come. "We could be in here for hours!"

Mandy was also beginning to think that the labyrinth was more difficult than she had expected. Maybe they weren't meant to see the tower, after all. "I don't mind if we don't reach the middle," she said. "It's more important that we find our way *out* before dark."

Beside her, Joanne shivered and looked anxious.

The path met another one and they were faced with a choice of going left or right. As Mandy hesitated, she felt a strong urge to go to the right. She turned along the narrow green path and spotted something darting around a bend just ahead of them. Was it the cat?

Mandy began to walk faster, anxious to see if her suspicions were correct. She rounded the corner at the end of the path, with James and Joanne close behind her, and saw a long slender shape vanishing through a gap in the hedge, not far ahead.

"It *is* the cat!" Mandy cried. "Quick! Let's try to catch up with it."

They charged along, every now and then catching glimpses of the cat whisking through a gap or turning down a new path. Mandy began to feel certain that it was showing them the way through the maze. But was the cat leading them out, or farther into the labyrinth?

At last, the path widened and they found themselves in a clearing. In the center stood the tower.

"This is it!" exclaimed Joanne triumphantly. "We've reached the middle. Good job, Mandy."

"*I* didn't find the way," said Mandy, looking around for the cat. It was nowhere to be seen.

James beckoned them through an archway that led into the tower. Inside, a winding stone staircase led them up to an open-air platform, from which they had a bird's-eye view of the complicated maze. Beyond the thick green hedges lay Wardour's beautiful gardens and the castle itself.

Mandy looked over the low parapet wall at the edge of the platform. When she saw the pattern of hedges below them, she realized that the maze wasn't in the traditional square shape at all. It was long and narrow with parts jutting out here and there. Suddenly it struck her that she was looking at the shape of a cat!

Mandy gasped. "We should have guessed that the design would feature a cat somehow," she said to James and Joanne as they peered over the wall beside her.

Mandy gazed over the distant trees and took a deep breath of fresh air. Just then, a soft whispering entered her head. *Look down*, it seemed to be saying.

Mandy shook her head, thinking she was hearing things. *Look down*, came the whisper again.

Mandy glanced down over the edge of the parapet. Far below, a brown leaf scudded across the ground at the foot of the tower. As it moved, it grew rounder and more solid, and Mandy found herself looking at a mouse scurrying across the grass.

"Look!" she cried in astonishment. "There's a mouse down there!" But even as James and Joanne looked around, the mouse grew flat and thin and Mandy was staring at a dead leaf again. She grinned at the others, feeling foolish. "False alarm," she said.

James shrugged and turned away and, with that, the strange whispering returned. *Look down*, it urged again.

At the bottom of the tower, several dry brown leaves were being blown across the grass. Mandy watched, cold with horror, as they transformed into big brown mice, running and swarming toward the tower. More and more streamed out of the hedges around the tower until Mandy could hardly see the grass between the packed brown bodies.

"Mandy, look at this." James's voice interrupted her, and Mandy jumped. The mice became leaves again, drifting quietly in the soft breeze.

Mandy turned to see James inspecting a plaque in the wall at the top of the stairs. On it was an engraving of the castle with its motto, FELES DEFENSOR. *Feles defensor*, thought Mandy. *"The cat is my protector." Protector against a plague of mice, perhaps? Did the cat in the maze bring her here to see a vision of what might happen if cats did not come back to the castle?*

Lying in bed that night, Mandy tossed and turned, trying to make sense of everything that had happened since she had arrived at Wardour. In her mind she replayed the strange noises and visions that had haunted her throughout the day.

But what exactly was going on? All Mandy knew for sure was that Wardour Castle was once proud of its cats but now they were no longer welcome. And there seemed to be phantom cats everywhere, filling Mandy's head with warnings about plagues of mice and appealing to her to do something to help them.

Wide awake, she rolled onto her back and stared up at the ceiling. *What about Fellows?* she wondered. *How much had he seen and what did he know? And as for Mrs. Hapgood,* she thought as she finally felt her eyes beginning to droop, *she acts really strange when anyone mentions a cat. Does she know that the castle is haunted?*

As these thoughts drifted through Mandy's mind, she became aware of a persistent tapping. It sounded like someone knocking on the windowpane. She looked across the room and, in the faint moonlight that trickled in through the narrow window, she saw the curtain rippling slightly, as if being blown by a breeze.

That's funny, Mandy thought. *I didn't leave the window open.*

She got up and went over to close it and to see what was making the noise. *Probably something down in the courtyard*, she told herself as she pushed the curtain aside.

But the window was shut tight. Not even a hint of a draft penetrated the glass pane. Yet, even as Mandy looked at it, the curtain billowed out again.

Mandy swallowed but her mouth felt dry. She tried to turn to go back to bed but found herself rooted to the spot. *What is going on here?* she appealed silently. Suddenly, she felt a strong urge to look out the window.

She leaned forward and looked down. Below, the courtyard was awash with moonlight. In the silvery brightness Mandy saw quite clearly a sleek, agile creature streaking across the paving stones in pursuit of a tiny shadow.

"It's a cat," she said out loud. "Chasing a mouse."

And behind her the room became filled with soft whisperings that seemed to say over and over again, *"Feles defensor, feles defensor."*

Mandy turned slowly, knowing for certain what she would see.

And there, sitting in the middle of the floor, was Puss, her ginger fur tinged with gold in the sparkling moonbeam that shone down on her through the window. In her green eyes there was the same yearning expression that Mandy had seen before, and the now-familiar sense of sadness and helplessness came from the little cat as she held Mandy in her gaze.

"Feles defensor, feles defensor" said the hushed echoes, and suddenly it all made sense to Mandy. Puss and the other cats Mandy had seen were the ghosts of the cats that used to roam so freely and happily at Wardour. And they couldn't rest until the castle became, in spirit, Castle Feles once more.

"What do you want me to do?" Mandy whispered.

Puss glided silently over to the door and, in a heartbeat, she vanished. Mandy rushed over and opened the door. Puss was in the hallway, waiting for her, just as she had done the night before. Mandy knew without hesitation that she had to follow. Puss ran along the hallway and down the stairs, but instead of turning toward the kitchen, the little cat continued across the great hall to the main entrance, then disappeared.

Mandy turned the big brass key and pulled the heavy door open. A blast of cold night air rushed in. She looked out and saw Puss sitting at the foot of one of the stone cat statues. The ghostly cat stood up as Mandy stepped outside, then she trotted soundlessly down the stairs.

Mandy stopped. "Just a minute, Puss!" she called out. "I'm going back for James. He'll help us, too."

She charged back up to her room, where she grabbed

a jacket and pulled on her shoes. Then she went through to James's room and shook him urgently. "Wake up, James. Wake up!" she whispered.

A few seconds later, Mandy was heading back down to the hall with James running behind her, struggling to pull a jacket on over his pajamas.

Outside, Puss was waiting at the bottom of the steps, where Mandy had left her. When the little cat saw them coming through the door, she flicked her tail and headed out into the night.

Seven

"Can you still see her, James?" asked Mandy. She had lost sight of Puss as a cloud drifted across the face of the moon, blocking out the soft glimmer that had lit up the little cat in front of them.

"No, it's too dark," said James. "Let's see if this helps." He reached into his pocket and brought out a slim flashlight not much bigger than a pen.

Mandy looked doubtfully at the narrow beam. "I suppose it's better than nothing," she said.

They came to the corner of the long guest wing. "Which way now?" Mandy asked.

The light from James's flashlight picked up a blur of

ginger that darted past a shrub and disappeared once more into the shadows. "That way," said James. "I think she's going toward the summerhouse."

They struck out across the lawn, the damp grass muffling their footsteps. Above them, the cloud drifted on, allowing the moon to light up the garden again. Bulky rhododendron bushes and thin, towering conifer trees cast eerie shadows across the lawn. Mandy shivered and felt glad that James was with her.

But there was no sign of the ghostly cat. "I wish Puss would stop vanishing like this," said James. "She's not making things very easy for us!"

They reached the summerhouse and sat on the swinging seat, hoping the cat would reappear. A pale shadow floated up from the ground nearby and merged with the frosty darkness of the night.

"Owl," Mandy whispered, trying to catch another glimpse of the bird on its soundless flight.

The slight swishing of the crisp leaves of a nearby oak tree was the only noise to be heard. In the brittle silence, the tiny rustle acted like a siren, giving the game away. Mandy looked up. The owl was perched on a branch, silhouetted against the unbroken blackness of the sky. And sitting calmly at the foot of the tree was Puss.

"Phew," said Mandy. "Come on, James!"

Puss's enormous green eyes flashed brightly at them before she turned and headed away from the castle.

Mandy and James started along the gravel path after her, their feet crunching noisily over the small stones. Mandy looked back at the gray bulk of the castle. "Let's stay on the grass," she suggested, wary of the sound their footsteps were making. She remembered how Fellows had surprised her in the kitchen. This time they had to make sure they didn't draw attention to themselves.

Ahead of them, a squat, square building loomed out of the darkness. It was the chapel Mandy had noticed earlier when they were looking at the architect's drawings of the castle. Puss was still visible in the moonlight, a darker shadow against the pale stone walls, but as soon as they neared the little building she faded from view again.

"She must have gone inside," said James. He walked across the graveyard to the porch. Not wanting to be left alone outside, Mandy followed him.

To her surprise, the door to the chapel was wide open. They tiptoed across the stone floor. The narrow beam from James's flashlight revealed a tiny, sparsely furnished chapel, with three or four rows of pews and an altar at the far end.

"Nothing here . . ." Mandy began, but then, out of nowhere, something swooped through the air down the short aisle and headed straight for her. Instinctively, she let out a sharp cry and ducked as the thing swerved to one side only inches in front of her, before it flicked through the door and out of sight.

Mandy let out a worried laugh. "Only a bat!" She grinned sheepishly as she spotted several more dark shapes flitting around the eaves of the steeply pitched roof.

"I hope they don't fly too close and get caught in our hair," said James warily.

Mandy shook her head. "That's an old wives' tale," she explained. "Bats are fantastic fliers and never crash into anything. They use sonar to tell where they're going. They won't hurt us."

"I hope not," said James, unsuccessfully trying to track the darting movements of one of the creatures with his flashlight.

They went farther along the aisle and glanced around. Apart from the bats, nothing disturbed the stillness. In the light of the flashlight, Mandy noticed that even here, the love of cats had influenced the decorations. The cushions were embroidered with pictures of cats and at the end of each pew was a carving of a cat's head.

"Even this candlestick is engraved with cats," she

pointed out, noticing an ornate gold candelabra on the altar.

"Well, I suppose the cats used to keep the chapel free of mice, too," said James. "But these carvings are the only cats in here now, because I can't see Puss anywhere."

"Yes. It looks like she's given us the slip again," said Mandy. Disappointed, she slumped into a pew. "And I was so sure she was leading us to something important in here." She sighed.

"Maybe she's in the graveyard," James suggested.

"The graveyard!" Mandy echoed. "That's a bit —" She broke off as a soft thud, like a footstep, sounded behind them. Before they could turn to see what it was, there came the sound of a distinct click.

"Who's there?" Mandy cried out, spinning around.

There was no reply — just a suspicion of someone fading into the shadows as the silence folded around them again.

"Someone's been following us," Mandy whispered, jumping up and hurrying to the door.

"Maybe it was another bat — or even a mouse," said James, scrambling after her.

Mandy stopped short. "I don't think so," she murmured slowly. "The door's been closed. I hope it's not locked." She had a sudden picture of them having to spend the rest of the night in the creepy chapel and wondered how long it would be before anyone found them there.

"There's only one way to find out," said James, pushing down the big iron handle.

To their relief, the door began to swing open.

"Wait!" Mandy whispered, darting forward and grabbing the handle firmly. "We can't just go barging out there if there's a prowler sneaking around. It might be dangerous."

"You're right," agreed James. "We'll have to be careful."

Inch by inch, he pushed the door open until there was a big enough gap for him to peer through.

Mandy stood on her toes and looked out over his head. "I can't see anything," she whispered.

"Me, neither," said James. "I think the coast's clear."

They slipped out into the open and waited. Nothing moved.

"It must have been the wind. . . ." said James, his voice trailing off as he caught Mandy's disbelieving expression.

"There isn't any wind," she pointed out, shaking her head slowly.

A haunting *whooo, whooo* from an overhanging yew tree spread out into the silence. It drifted on the air until another owl hooted its melancholy reply from the other side of the graveyard.

"Something's moving," James said fearfully. "Over there. Look!" He pointed down the path that led around the chapel.

Mandy caught a glimpse of a tall dark shape slipping behind a gravestone. "What was that?" she asked, her voice a hoarse croak.

"A man, I think." James took a breath.

They waited in silence but the mysterious figure did not emerge from its hiding place.

"We can't stand here all night," said Mandy. She took a deep breath, summoning up enough courage to investigate. After all, whoever it was had made no attempt to approach them, so he probably meant them no harm. "Let's go and see who's there."

They approached the gravestone cautiously.

"Anyone there?" Mandy called out, trying to sound calm.

There was no answer. She crept forward, then jumped back in alarm as a sleek shape with a bushy tail shot out from behind the worn gravestone.

"Oh!" James gasped as it flew past them, then hurtled down the path and vanished into the inky night.

"It's only a fox!" Mandy laughed. "And it probably got

a much bigger fright than we did. So much for your man, James!"

"But I could have sworn I saw someone," said James, puzzled. He walked around to the front of the grave for a closer look. Folding his arms, he shook his head slowly. "And foxes don't stand upright, or leave footprints." He bent down and shone the flashlight on a clear outline in the chalky mud. It was of a man's boot.

"How do we know it's a fresh print?" Mandy pointed out. "It could have been made earlier in the day."

James straightened up. "I guess you're right," he said. "It must have just been the fox that I saw."

As he stood up, the ray of light from his flashlight lit up the gravestone in front of them. Mandy saw that it was decorated with an elaborate pattern of tiny cats running endlessly around the edge of the stone. She peered closer and read out loud the inscription on the stone. *Here lies the body of Joe Turner. Born 19th May 1890 and died of the scarlet fever on 8th August 1902.*

Mandy's heart began to beat rapidly as the chiseled-out words began to sink in. She continued: *A much loved son and nephew and a faithful friend to all the cats.*

She read the words on the stone again. "James!" she gasped. "We've found the grave of the boy I saw in the kitchen! He was about twelve years old, and Fellows called him Joe!"

Here lies the body of Joe Turner. Born 10 May 1890 and died of the scarlet fever on 8th August 1902. A much loved son and nephew and a faithful friend to all the cats.

Mandy remembered the way Joe had looked at her before he disappeared — friendly but sad as well, with the same sense of appealing to Mandy that Puss had. "I think he needs our help, too," Mandy declared. "And there's only one way to find out." She turned and sped off down the path. "Come on, James! There's no time to lose."

"What do you mean?" James called, running after her.

"It's nearly midnight!" Mandy shouted back over her shoulder. "And that's when I saw Joe last night. We have to go to the kitchen and see if we can meet him again."

"But what do you think he can tell us?" James asked, catching up with her.

"I'm not sure," said Mandy, running faster. "But I'm sure he wants something from us. Maybe he can't rest until cats are brought back to Wardour again. And the only way that will happen is if Mrs. Hapgood learns how important they once were. Perhaps Joe knows where the documents are and is waiting for a chance to tell someone where to find them. . . ."

Eight

A faint scuttling noise greeted them as they quietly pushed open the scullery door. James hastily switched off the flashlight just in case anyone was awake and spotted the beam.

Mandy hesitated, trying to make out what the sound was. "That could be Joe and the cats," she whispered. "Perhaps they're in here tonight."

She held her breath, expecting the ghostly group to appear before them.

But the darkness of the cold stone room remained unbroken. Mandy couldn't *see* any ghosts. But she was sure there was *something* in the room with them.

The scrambling sounds stopped and in their place came a steady *drip, drip, drip.*

Mandy began, taking a step forward. "Let's go —" But she stopped dead as the echoing silence was suddenly filled with a pattering, scrabbling noise.

A sharp intake of breath sounded behind her. "Whaaa —" James gasped. "Something just ran over my feet!" He switched on the flashlight, revealing a floor that was alive with half a dozen big brown mice bolting across the ground in search of cover. Two of them leaped into the ancient cooking pot in the fireplace, while three others scampered behind the dishwasher. Within seconds they had vanished, leaving behind a ravaged scene of vegetable peel and dirty plastic bags. Mandy groaned as she imagined how horrified Mrs. Hapgood and Mrs. Moore would be if they could see the scullery now. On the drain board next to the sink, a green glass bottle lay on its side, dripping thick yellow oil onto the tiles.

"We'd better clean this up," said James, putting his flashlight on a table and setting an overturned pail upright before squatting down to pick up the scattered garbage.

Mandy bent down to help him. But then a thought struck her. "Wait. Let's leave it," she said. "Mrs. Hapgood should see this."

James looked at her, frowning slightly. Mandy could tell he thought she had gone crazy. Then his face cleared, and he nodded in agreement. "Of course! More proof that cats are important to Wardour," he said, dropping a sticky bag back onto the floor.

Upstairs, the faint chime of a grandfather clock began to strike the hour. "Midnight!" Mandy exclaimed. "If Joe's going to appear, it'll be now. Come on. Let's go."

They stepped over the trash and tiptoed toward the kitchen door.

"I hope he keeps regular hours," said James, "or we could be in for a long wait!"

"I don't think you have to worry about that. He's there, all right." Mandy breathed as the sound of Joe greeting his beloved cats came from behind the kitchen door.

"Hello again, my beauties," he was crooning. "Have you been catching mice for your friend Joe?"

Mandy felt a chill run down her spine. She tried to remind herself that Joe had seemed friendly the last time she saw him, but suddenly the room felt cold. Mandy could hear her heart thudding in her chest. Then she thought of Puss's face, her green eyes desperate and pleading.

Mandy took a deep breath and pushed down the door handle. *I can't believe I'm about to offer help to a ghost!* she thought to herself.

Behind her, James stepped forward. He stopped and stared in amazement at the scene before him. The boy from another century stood in the center of the floor, softly illuminated by the moonlight that shone through the high kitchen windows. He was surrounded by several purring cats, who looked up at him lovingly as they wound themselves around his ankles. And in his arms was Puss, gazing steadily at Mandy and James with her huge emerald eyes.

James breathed out slowly.

Joe turned his head and looked at them, and Mandy recognized the gentle but sorrowful expression on his face. At the same time, Puss jumped down from his arms and slipped across to Mandy and curled around her legs. Mandy realized with a jolt that she couldn't actually *feel* the little cat's body — just a waft of warm air, like someone breathing on her skin.

Puss wove herself between Mandy's feet once more, then trotted back to Joe, who picked her up and beckoned to Mandy and James.

Mandy caught her breath. *He does want to show us something*, she thought. She turned to James. "Perhaps he's going to lead us to the secret room," she whispered.

With Puss at his heels, Joe moved silently out of the kitchen and headed toward the stairs leading to the entrance hall. The other cats faded away as soon as he was out of sight. Mandy and James exchanged a look of excitement, then hurried across the kitchen after him.

The dim lamp at the foot of the stairs gave off just enough light for Mandy to be able to make out Joe's dark shadow flitting ahead of her and James. She wondered if they should switch on the flashlight to make sure they didn't bump into anything, but then she remembered that James had left it on the table in the scullery. It was too late to go back for it now. They would just have to rely on Joe to lead them in the dark.

Mandy and James cautiously tiptoed up the kitchen stairs and across the entrance hall. Joe was waiting for them at the door to the dining room, a pale shape just visible among the shadows. He slipped inside as soon as they caught up with him.

"Do you think the secret chamber is in here, after all?" whispered James as they followed Joe through the heavy wooden door.

"I don't know how it can be," said Mandy. "We searched every corner."

"Yes, but don't forget, I'm sure there was an extra window somewhere around here," James pointed out.

Joe was standing in the middle of the room, illuminated by the soft silver moonlight. His freckled face seemed kind. Even though Joe looked very serious now, Mandy could imagine his blue eyes twinkling with mischief.

Joe beckoned them over to one of the windows. For a moment, Mandy thought he was about to pass through it, but he stopped and pointed down at the window seat.

"We can't sit down now," muttered Mandy. "There's not much time. . . ." She trailed off as Joe pointed urgently at the cushion. Mandy frowned as she tried to make sense of Joe's signals. Then she gasped and clutched at James. "James, do you think the window seat is the way into the secret room?" she asked breathlessly.

Joe's face lit up with a beaming smile. Then, without another sign to them, he vanished.

Mandy and James ran across the room and pulled off the thick, embroidered cushion. With both hands, Mandy carefully lifted up the heavy seat top. It opened easily on well-oiled hinges, and they found themselves staring down into a black hole. The air in the hole smelled musty and stale. Mandy swallowed hard. She looked at James, and he gave her a short nod of encouragement.

Taking a deep breath, she squeezed into the narrow opening, her heart thudding in her chest. Her feet found a hard, smooth ledge, and she realized that she was at the top of a ladder. Slowly, she swung one leg down until her foot came to rest on another foothold, and soon she was cautiously making her way down into the soft blackness.

Above her, she could hear James following her. The ancient wooden ladder creaked and swayed under their combined weight.

"Be careful!" she gasped, hearing a loud crack. What if the ladder broke? How far would they fall? Would they be able to climb out again?

Grasping the sides of the ladder firmly, Mandy paused. There was another alarming snap. She winced and held her breath, certain that they were about to go plummeting down to the bottom — wherever that was. Then something hard hit her head. "Ouch!" she cried.

"Sorry!" James called softly. "I didn't know that was you."

"Don't worry," Mandy replied. "I shouldn't have stopped." She lowered her foot down and stepped onto solid floorboards. She had been only one rung up from the bottom. "Keep going!" she called up to James. "You've got only a few steps to go."

"It's really stuffy in here," James complained, trying to draw a deep breath as he felt his way to the bottom of the ladder.

Mandy blinked and looked around her. A glimmer of moonlight was filtering through a tiny window, revealing a square room that was hardly bigger than Mandy's bathroom. The walls were bare plaster lined with sturdy wooden beams, and the floor was made of uneven floorboards. At first sight, the room was completely empty. Mandy's heart sank. Why had Joe brought them down here?

Another ominous creaking sounded above them.

Mandy's mouth went dry. She grabbed the ladder, hoping it wasn't about to collapse, but it stood strongly against the wall and seemed capable of holding out for a few more centuries. Then, as Mandy's eyes became accustomed to the gray light, she noticed something that made her heart leap. On the floor, in the cramped corner behind the steps, was an old wooden chest.

She dropped to her knees and dragged it out with James's help. A big, rusty padlock held the lid in place. Mandy tugged at it, hoping it would give way, but it was locked. "Where's the key?" she cried, feeling frustrated. She was sure the cat documents were in the chest, but she couldn't see a way in.

James gave the padlock a mighty jerk, but it held fast. He let go and it clattered against the wooden box. "I suppose the only thing we can do is carry it out of here," he said despondently. "But it won't be easy hauling a heavy chest up that ladder."

Mandy felt a breath of warm air above her. She

glanced up. "I don't think we'll have to," she said to James with a smile.

Joe was sitting on the steps above them with Puss curled in his arms. He grinned down at them as he smoothed Puss's soft ginger coat. Then he moved silently down the ladder and bent over the chest. He looked sideways at them, and Mandy thought she saw a mischievous expression on his pale face. With the faintest of smiles turning up the corners of his mouth, Joe passed his hand effortlessly through the lock, breaking its clasp.

James burst out laughing. "I think he was showing off," he said. He pulled the broken padlock off and carefully lifted the lid.

The chest was filled with dozens of yellowing, rolled-up documents. Mandy picked one up and spread it out on the floor under the window. James knelt down beside her, and they carefully examined the document in the pool of faint moonlight. Joe stood beside him, still holding Puss, who was looking down at them curiously.

In the center of the curling sheet of paper, there was a detailed drawing of a very familiar cat. Mandy's eyes were drawn to the bold heading at the top. *Puss*, it read. *Mother to many and a legendary hunter. One of the best.*

Mandy glanced up and her eyes met the soft, green

gaze of Puss. "You're famous!" she said in admiration. "I always knew you were special." She smiled.

"Listen to this!" James's eager voice broke into her thoughts. He had unrolled another document and was holding it flat on the dusty floor.

"What does it say?" asked Mandy, crawling across to join him.

James began to read aloud. "*Castle Feles is named after its colony of faithful cats that defended it through the ages against plagues of mice,*" he read. "*Before the first family of cats arrived, the rodents spread diseases amongst the inhabitants, destroyed the crops in the barns, and pillaged the food in the kitchens. There was little that man could do to ward off this pest. Traps and poison were to no avail.*"

"Mrs. Hapgood will *have* to read this," said Mandy.

As James read on, the importance of the cats became even clearer: "*Without the spirited little hunters, the castle would have been ruined — just as the surrounding farms had been. When the farmers saw how Castle Feles had survived the rodent plague, they, too, began to welcome cats into their homes. The castle's owners donated some kittens from their colony to their neighbors and, within a few generations, the cats had helped to restore the adjoining properties, too.*"

"And now the mice are on the march again," James

announced, sitting back on his heels. "If Mrs. Hapgood doesn't do something soon, the castle could be swamped by them all over again."

"But this information will help," Mandy pointed out. "When Mrs. Hapgood sees how cats have looked after the castle for centuries, she's bound to change her mind about having them in the castle."

They replaced the documents in the trunk and closed the heavy lid. Mandy yawned as she stood up. "We'd better get some sleep now," she said. "We've got a lot of explaining to do in the morning."

"I just hope Mrs. Hapgood is pleased with our discovery," said James.

They climbed back up to the dining room where, to Mandy's surprise, Joe was waiting for them. She had imagined he would have left them, now that they had the evidence they needed.

"We'll be all right now, Joe," said Mandy, lowering the lid of the window seat. "We're going to put things right for you and the cats."

But Joe hovered by the door. Puss regarded them with her huge green eyes from her snug place in his arms. Mandy could see Joe was reluctant to go. Was there something else he wanted them to do?

"I promise you we'll tell Mrs. Hapgood everything," Mandy tried to reassure him.

Joe held up a hand. Then he stared hard at Mandy and slipped through the door.

In a flash, Mandy understood. Joe hadn't finished yet. Without hesitation, she strode after him. "We're not off to bed yet," she whispered loudly to James. "I think Joe wants to show us something else."

Nine

Mandy heard the grandfather clock striking just once as she sped out into the entrance hall with James hard on her heels. The pale figure of Joe lingered briefly by the front door before fading through the solid oak panels.

"It must be handy to be able to do that!" James said in surprise, the sound of his voice echoing around the empty area.

"We might have to disappear as well if we make any more noise," said Mandy as their sneakers squeaked loudly on the polished marble floor.

They slipped through the front door, then quietly pulled it closed behind them. Mandy was relieved to be outside where there was less chance of being heard. If she and James were caught now, they might never find out what Joe wanted to show them.

Joe and Puss were waiting next to one of the stone cats. As soon as Mandy and James were outside, they drifted down the steps and trotted soundlessly along the gravel path in front of the castle in the direction of the keep.

"I wonder where he's taking us," said James, panting, while running alongside Mandy as they tried to catch up with Joe.

"We'll find out very soon." Mandy gasped for breath. "At this rate, we'll probably break some kind of speed record!"

Even though they were running as fast as they could, they were barely gaining on Joe, whose shadowy figure was just visible ahead of them.

"It must be really urgent," James puffed.

Joe flitted past the keep and struck out across the lawns that stretched away from the castle.

"He's going toward the fields," said James.

Soon they had left the neatly trimmed lawns and were heading across open fields that were covered with a crisp white mantle of frost. Mandy shivered in the icy air, even though she'd been running hard. "I wish I was wearing more than just this jacket and my pajamas," she said.

James didn't answer, for they had come to a hedge and he was busy finding a path through them. They jumped down into the next field and spotted Joe slipping between the haystacks on the far side. A bulky shape loomed up against the sky ahead of him.

"Isn't that a barn over there?" asked James, squinting into the darkness.

They ran across the field of stubble, their feet swishing and crunching against the crisp straw stalks. As they drew nearer to the barn, Mandy looked around for their ghostly guide. There was no sign of him. "Where did he go?" she wondered aloud.

"He must be inside," said James.

They made their way around to the open end of the barn. In the gray moonlight, Mandy could make out just how ramshackle the place was. Inside, the barn was full of thick shadows, and the air smelled damp. The only sound was their noisy breathing. Mandy glanced briefly at James, his face a pale disk beside her. Then she took a deep breath and stepped into the barn.

After a few moments, her eyes got used to the darkness. She picked her way carefully around a rusting pile of farm implements. Mandy wondered if some of these pieces of ancient machinery had been around in the happy days when the cats had protected the harvest.

"It's pretty cold in here," James muttered behind her. Mandy heard him clap his hands together to get warm.

Just then, Mandy spotted Joe waiting for them at the far end of the barn. Moonlight seeped in through a hole in the wall, illuminating his red hair. As Mandy and James reached him, he turned and slipped effortlessly up a ladder that led to a hayloft running across one half of the barn.

After giving the ladder a quick tug to check that it was secure, Mandy and James climbed up after him. At the top, a scattering of loose hay covered the floor and in one corner it had been pushed up into a heap.

Joe was already sitting on the pile of hay. Mandy noticed with a thrill that his skinny body made no imprint on the dry stalks. He was gazing down at something beside him, a warm smile lighting up his face. Puss sat next to him, also staring intently into the hay.

"What are they looking at?" Mandy whispered to James.

Joe glanced up and put a finger to his lips, then pointed down at the hay.

Mandy and James crept over. As they leaned forward, Mandy thought she spotted something stirring. At the same time, she heard a very faint growl.

Mandy knelt down and peered into the hay. "Look, James!" she said breathlessly.

In the snug nest lay a living, breathing ginger cat. With her enormous green eyes and beautiful dark ginger stripes, she could have been Puss's twin. And curled up with her were five tiny kittens — two ginger, two tabby, and a dusky black one.

Mandy's heart skipped a beat. She hardly dared to breathe as the mother cat lifted her head and stared distrustfully at the two newcomers. In a soft, reassuring voice, Mandy said, "We're your friends." She glanced at James, who was crouching down next to her. "Aren't they gorgeous?" she whispered.

James nodded and looked closer at the little family. "They seem very young," he said. "Too young to be in this cold old barn."

"Yes, they're only about a week old," Mandy guessed. She wanted to pick up one of the kittens to make sure, but she knew this would upset the mother even further.

An icy draft whooshed in through a hole in the roof above them and wrapped itself around the group in the loft.

James looked up at the hole. "This hay must get soaked when it rains," he observed.

"You're right," Mandy agreed. "But if no one ever

comes here, it's probably the only place where she felt safe enough to have her kittens," she added sadly.

The mother cat stretched as two of the kittens nuzzled closer to her, and Mandy noticed with concern how thin she was. With five young babies to feed and keep warm, she probably had little chance to go out hunting for food. "Things must be really tough for her right now," said Mandy, feeling a lump form in her throat.

She looked up. Joe was staring anxiously at her as if he were waiting for her to do something.

With a jolt, Mandy realized why Joe had brought them there. "Of course." She breathed in. "Joe wants us to take them back to the castle, where they can be warm and dry and properly cared for."

"You could be right," said James, beside her. "This means Joe hasn't just been taking care of the cats from the past. He's also been keeping watch over the living cats."

Mandy thought about this for a moment. "I think Joe and Puss have been waiting all along for this mother and her litter to be allowed to live safely inside the castle."

Mandy looked again at Joe, the guardian of the cats, and this time his blue eyes met hers with an expression of complete joy.

But the full responsibility of their task was beginning to dawn on Mandy. It was no longer simply a matter of showing the documents to Mrs. Hapgood to make her understand how important cats were to the history of Wardour Castle. For here was a little group of real, live cats that needed a good home immediately. "And not just any home," Mandy murmured. She stared into the huge green eyes of the mother cat and recognized quite clearly the identical gaze of Puss. "You know what, James?" she whispered. "I think these are the descendants of Puss!" The mother and her kittens belonged to Wardour and always had!

"I thought they looked alike — the ginger kittens even have the same dark stripes," James agreed, leaning forward to get a better look at them.

"Careful," Mandy whispered. "We mustn't make her feel threatened."

But the mother cat was no longer eyeing them suspiciously. She blinked at James, then closed her eyes and began to purr loudly to show how proud she was of her five beautiful babies.

Mandy reached out slowly and stroked her head. The little animal purred louder and stretched out her neck. Mandy noticed that she wasn't, in fact, an exact replica of Puss. On her chest was a distinctive white V-shape.

"Hey!" exclaimed James, also spotting the white marking. "We've seen her before. Isn't she the cat we saw at the maze yesterday?"

"I think so," said Mandy. She remembered the cat she'd glimpsed dashing across the courtyard just before Puss visited her that night. Had it been the mother cat hunting for mice?

"So it looks like there's been a real cat prowling around the castle, after all," said James.

Mandy gently scratched the purring mother's neck, feeling the vibration in her throat. She hoped it wouldn't be too long before the friendly little cat was in a warm, safe place with plenty of food.

One of the ginger kittens was snuffling about in the straw. Mandy reached out with one finger and rubbed its soft fur. She kept a close eye on the mother cat, because she didn't want to upset her. But the adult cat didn't seem to mind. It looked as if she had begun to trust Mandy and James already.

Mandy gently picked up the kitten and held it close to her face, breathing in its sweet, milky scent. "Don't worry, little one, you'll be OK now," she promised. "I'm sure you'll grow up to be a king — or a queen — of the castle," she added softly.

She handed the kitten to James, who cupped it in his hands and studied its rich ginger coat. "This one really *does* look like Puss," he said. "If anything is proof that these are her direct descendants, it's this little thing."

"Which means that if Mrs. Hapgood lets them stay at the castle, then Puss will live on at Wardour," said Mandy in a hushed voice.

She looked up to see Joe's reaction. The ghostly boy dipped his head solemnly, and Mandy read in his gesture a signal that they were right. But his face was still filled with desperate longing as he looked down again at the living cats in their nest of hay. A longing to see the family safely established in the castle, so that he and his colony of long-past cats could finally be at peace.

Ten

"Your mom looks a bit flustered," Mandy said to Joanne at breakfast later that morning.

Mrs. Moore was bustling about the dining room, her face red and a worried look in her eyes.

"She's in a rush because she had to clean up a mess in the scullery before she could start cooking breakfast," Joanne explained. She dropped her voice. "She thinks there were mice in there last night."

Mandy grinned at James, then whispered to Joanne, "She might not have to clean up after them again."

Joanne frowned at her. "What do you mean?"

"We saw the cats again last night," Mandy told her. "And they might be coming back to Wardour for real."

Joanne's mouth dropped. "How do you know?" she asked.

But Mandy couldn't explain any more because Fellows was offering them each a glass of orange juice. "Late night?" He raised his eyebrows meaningfully as Mandy struggled to hide a yawn.

Mandy grinned at him. It had been more than just a late night. By the time she and James had crept back to their rooms, the sky was already growing lighter. She felt as if her head had hardly touched the pillow before her dad was knocking on her door, warning her she was going to be late for breakfast.

A sliding noise announced the arrival of the dumbwaiter. Mrs. Moore and Fellows walked across to the wooden panels, opened them, and lifted out some delicious-smelling dishes of food. One of the plates was full of sizzling bacon. Mandy remembered her plan to sneak some out for the mystery cat and hoped that she wouldn't have to now. If all went well, the little family in the barn would soon be happily settled in their rightful home.

She looked across at Mrs. Hapgood, who was sitting at the head of the table. Would they be able to persuade her to change her mind about the cats?

Mrs. Hapgood caught her eye and smiled broadly.

I don't think she'd look so happy if she knew what's been going on, thought Mandy, returning the smile.

Mrs. Hapgood turned to the other guests. "How did you all get on with the mystery? Does anyone have any interesting information for us?" she asked.

Mandy decided that it was now or never. There was too much at stake to waste any more time. The kittens needed a warm, dry bed and the mother needed some nourishing food. She stood up quickly. "We do," she announced confidently.

A murmur of surprise broke out as everyone looked up expectantly.

"We've got something very important to tell you all," Mandy continued. "Haven't we, James?"

James nodded and stood up next to her.

"Don't tell me you two have solved the mystery ahead of everyone!" Dr. Adam smiled at them both as he sat back and folded his arms.

Mandy returned her father's smile. "We've discovered something pretty amazing," she said. Then, unable to resist teasing him, she added, "I don't think you'd have cracked this one in a million years, Dad — even dressed as Sherlock Holmes!"

Dr. Adam laughed good-naturedly. "OK. So I'm not much of a detective."

"No, but it's good that you're a vet," Mandy replied, picturing the tiny kittens and their hungry mother out in the barn.

Mrs. Hapgood looked puzzled. She glanced at Fellows and raised her eyebrows as if he might know what was going on.

But Fellows merely shook his head and shrugged his shoulders.

"So, what is it you youngsters have found?" Mr. Russell boomed out jovially. "Come on, impress us all."

Mandy took a deep breath. "We've discovered the true history of Wardour Castle," she said slowly, allowing time for her words to sink in.

"The history of this place?" said Mr. Russell, taken aback. "What's that got to do with the stolen candelabra?"

"Nothing," James told him.

"Nothing?" echoed Dr. Emily. "So why the interest in history?"

"Because it's much more important than the made-up mystery," Mandy declared. She looked solemnly at Mrs. Hapgood. "It could really make a big difference to Wardour. You see," and she cleared her throat nervously, "some lives depend on it." She hesitated, then added quietly. "The lives of a family of very special cats."

Mrs. Hapgood grew pale. "Of course I know there

used to be cats at Wardour," she said in a controlled tone. "But there are no cats here now, so it's not important."

"Oh, but it *is*," Mandy insisted. She longed to tell everyone all about the cat and her kittens in the barn, but she suspected it was too early. First they had to show Mrs. Hapgood the historical documents.

"There's something you might want to see, Mrs. Hapgood," said Mandy. She stepped out from the table and, with James, went across to the window seat.

"Please, could you all come over here?" James asked politely, beckoning to the bewildered guests.

With some murmurs of confusion, the guests stood up and shuffled across the carpet. Mandy and James glanced at each other, then lifted up the lid of the window seat to reveal the entrance to the secret room.

There were cries of amazement as people stared down into the black hole.

"What on earth is that?" gasped Mrs. Hapgood.

Dr. Adam was peering intently into the hole. "There's a ladder inside," he said. "Where does it go?"

"To a secret chamber," James told him. He climbed confidently inside and soon disappeared from view.

Mandy looked around at the stunned faces. Fellows was standing just behind Mrs. Hapgood, beaming broadly. As his eyes met Mandy's he winked, then, with a casualness that was rather out of character for the formal butler, he lifted his thumb as if to say, "Well done."

Mandy mirrored the gesture. She turned back to Mrs. Hapgood and said, "There are some important documents down there."

"What are they about?" Mrs. Hapgood asked faintly. She still looked pale and shocked. She clearly had no idea what lay beneath the seat.

"Cats that were heroes," said Mandy simply.

Before Mrs. Hapgood could reply, Mandy swung her legs over the edge of the window seat and stepped down onto the top rung of the ladder. She reached down to James, who was already on his way back up with an armful of slippery documents. He handed one of the scrolls to Mandy, and she climbed back out and gave it to Mrs. Hapgood.

There was a hushed silence as Mrs. Hapgood unrolled the ancient document on the dining table and began to read. Once or twice she shook her head, while Mandy looked on anxiously, wondering what was going through the woman's mind.

Without saying a word, Mrs. Hapgood gave the scroll back to Mandy, then took another one from James, who had climbed out of the window seat and was waiting next to her, a pile of scrolls in his arms.

One by one, Mrs. Hapgood went through them all.

Then she looked up and smiled at Mandy. "Well, it all makes for interesting reading, but I can't see what use this can be to Wardour," she said, sounding rather defensive.

"Because people will be fascinated by it," said Mandy. "You'll get even more people staying here now, because it makes the castle different from anywhere else."

Mrs. Hapgood stiffened. "I'm not sure you really know about these things, Mandy," she said and then folded her arms in front of her chest.

Meanwhile, some of the guests had begun to take the scrolls from James and spread them out on the table to read.

"This is extraordinary!" Dr. Emily exclaimed, admiring the drawing of Puss. "Normally, castles are protected by knights in shining armor. Not cats!"

"And as for this hidden room," said Mr. Russell, peering into the narrow opening, "I've got to have a look in there."

"Me, too," echoed several of the other guests, crowding around the window seat.

"Well," Mandy began hesitantly. She looked at her father and Mr. Russell. "Some of you might find it a bit of a tight squeeze going down the ladder."

"Never!" Dr. Adam laughed and climbed into the window seat, with Mr. Russell following close behind.

The two men made their way carefully down to the room. Mandy could hear them walking around on the bare floorboards and exclaiming over the old chest. They came back up, shaking their heads in amazement.

"Quite fascinating!" Mr. Russell pronounced. "And such a privilege to be one of the first guests to see it." He beamed at Mrs. Hapgood. "No doubt this will become a regular feature in your weekend mysteries."

Mrs. Hapgood still had her arms folded tightly in front of her, her head held stiffly at a slight angle, but now she seemed to be listening to what Mr. Russell was saying. She dropped her arms loosely to her sides and turned to face him. Mandy held her breath. What was Mrs. Hapgood going to say?

"Do you know, I think you have a good point there." Mrs. Hapgood smiled at Mr. Russell. "I will certainly think about it." She peered down into the hole. "I wonder why this was built?" she pondered. "People are bound to want to know."

"I think the most likely explanation is that it was a priests' hole," Dr. Adam suggested. "This castle is certainly old enough. But what *I* would like to know," he went on, frowning at Mandy, "is how you found out about it in the first place."

Mandy thought for a moment. Would anyone believe her if she told them how Joe and Puss had led her there? *Probably not*, she decided. *They'd think I was just making it all up.* "It was James's idea, really," she said to her father. "He thought we should count the windows in the castle and compare them with the map in the library. That's how we discovered that there was an extra one, which must have been a secret room."

"I'd read about it somewhere," James put in, grinning sideways at Mandy. "We just got lucky, I suppose."

"Mmm, lucky indeed," said Dr. Emily. "Because you certainly unearthed some very important documents. I wonder who hid them here in the first place?"

"That's what I'd like to know, too," said Mandy, glancing at Fellows.

The butler gave her the slightest of smiles, then shrugged his shoulders and turned away. Mandy frowned. If it *had* been Fellows, then surely he would have shown them where the room was right at the beginning. Or would he? If Mrs. Hapgood had known about his involvement, then maybe his job would have been in danger. Mandy realized that the answer would always remain a secret. It wasn't important, as long as the truth was out and the cats could be saved.

"I don't think that really matters now," broke in Mrs. Hapgood breezily. She had scooped up an armful of the papers and was cradling them protectively. "The important thing is to have these documents checked out by historians. I'm going to take them to the local museum first thing in the morning." She smiled at Mandy and James. "Who knows, this might just help to put Wardour on the map in quite a big way!" Then, quietly, she added, "It's just as well I haven't thrown out *all* of the cat memorabilia."

A wave of relief surged through Mandy. This was just what she wanted! If Mrs. Hapgood was this pleased to find out about the history of her castle, then there was a chance she would be willing to give a home to the family in the barn. Mandy took a deep breath. It was time to tell her about them.

Mandy cleared her throat. "There's something else we have to show you," she said. "And this is even more important than the documents."

Everyone looked at her and waited.

"You see," Mandy went on, "there aren't only documents and statues of cats at Wardour." She looked directly at Mrs. Hapgood. "There are real ones here, too."

"*Real* ones! Here — at Wardour?" said Mrs. Hapgood, a look of astonishment on her face.

Mandy nodded. "Yes, but they don't actually live *in* the castle." In a lower voice, she added, "Not yet, anyway." She went over to the door of the dining room and held it open invitingly. "Come with us and we'll show you."

With Mandy and James leading the way, Mrs. Hapgood and her guests tramped across the fields toward the barn. The frost of the night before had evaporated in the soft autumn sunshine. Joanne skipped happily alongside Mandy and James. Mandy looked at her and smiled. Joanne had obviously guessed they were going to see the cats Mandy had told her about earlier that morning.

As they reached the barn, Mandy asked the guests to wait by the door so that they wouldn't alarm the little family in the loft. Then she and James took Mrs. Hapgood and Mandy's mom and dad to the ladder at the back of the barn.

"May I come, too?" came Joanne's voice from behind them.

"Of course," said Mandy, beckoning to her.

Mandy and James went up the ladder first, then watched as Mrs. Hapgood climbed awkwardly up to the loft in her narrow black skirt. At the top, she straightened her skirt and looked around. "Well?" she said. "What am I supposed to be looking at up here?" She seemed puzzled by the strange location.

Dr. Adam and Dr. Emily climbed up the ladder, helping Joanne with the steep steps. They stood quietly at the edge of the loft, waiting for Mandy to show them what to do.

Mandy walked over to the pile of hay. There was a fierce draft whistling around the loft, and the mother cat had curled her thin body around her kittens in an effort to keep them warm. As Mandy looked into the nest, the cat looked up at her and gave a soft meow of recognition. Mandy turned to Mrs. Hapgood and waved her over.

Mrs. Hapgood stepped carefully across the uneven wooden floor. As soon as she saw the nest of kittens, she breathed in sharply. Then she turned to Mandy, looking regretful. "I'm sorry, Mandy," she said. "They'll have to go. We can't have all these cats."

Mandy's heart sank. How could Mrs. Hapgood be so interested in the history of her castle but still reject the cats living here now?

"But they're the direct descendants of the cats that saved the castle," James pointed out. "They *belong* here. They're part of the history," he finished persuasively.

"How can you be sure of that?" asked Mrs. Hapgood, picking a piece of hay off her blouse.

Mandy crouched down next to the nest of cats. She was determined to remain calm, because she knew she stood no chance of changing Mrs. Hapgood's mind if she showed her frustration. "Look at the mother's dark ginger stripes," she said, pulling aside the hay to reveal the mother cat's body. "She's identical to the paintings of the cats on your dishes."

"And to the drawing of Puss in that document you saw earlier," James added.

"And they've all got the same big green eyes," said Joanne. She was kneeling down at the edge of the pile of hay and was softly stroking the thin little cat.

Mandy suddenly thought of something else. "You know, if they *are* Puss's descendants," she said, "it's just goes to show how loyal they are to their home because, even though they weren't allowed in the castle anymore, they didn't go very far away."

A voice came up to them from the ground. "What have you found up there?"

Mandy looked down.

Mr. Russell was at the bottom of the ladder. "Everyone is anxious to find out what's going on," he said.

"Come and see, then you can tell them," Mandy invited. The mother cat seemed quite used to visitors now, so one more probably wouldn't make any difference.

When Mr. Russell saw the little family, he crouched down and grinned. "Oh, aren't they handsome!" Then, looking more closely at the mother cat, he said, "Do you know something? I think I've seen you before!" He looked up at Mandy. "I could have sworn I saw a little ginger cat scampering down the hallway ahead of me the other morning, but I thought I must have been imagining things." He raised his eyebrows meaningfully at Mrs. Hapgood.

Mrs. Hapgood sighed. "It would appear that a number of people *have* seen her," she said, "judging from other mentions of a ginger cat. I might even have — er — seen her myself once or twice," she admitted. "But I had to think of my guests, you know. Not everyone wants to share a house with pets!"

"Well, I can't speak for everyone," said Mr. Russell, "but I know I love to have animals around me, especially when I'm on vacation!"

"Yes, and what about Mr. and Mrs. Hitch?" Mandy burst out. "They didn't want to stay at all if they had to leave Archie behind." She fell silent as her mother gave her a stern look.

"Well, it certainly looks as if this cat's used to people," said Dr. Emily, stepping forward to take a closer look at the nest. "I don't think you'd have any problems bringing them into a house," she pointed out, as Joanne picked up the black kitten while its mother lay on her side, purring proudly.

"But even though they're so tame, they'll still have all

their hunting instincts — just like their famous ancestors," James added.

Mandy smiled at her friend. He'd just given her the lead she needed. "I bet there aren't a lot of mice in here!" she said. "And the cats could definitely deal with any that came to live in the castle."

Mrs. Hapgood looked unconvinced. "Poison and traps work just as well," she stated firmly. Through narrow eyes, she stared at the snuffling, furry bundles in the hay.

A heavy silence fell on the group in the loft. Mandy clenched her fists tightly, her nails digging into the palms of her hands. What if Mrs. Hapgood refused to allow the cats to stay? Then everything would have been in vain and Joe and Puss would never be able to rest in peace.

Her father looked across at Mandy and gave her a quick smile. He seemed to have guessed what she was thinking. "You know, I think these cats could have a very big role to play in the castle," he said, tugging thoughtfully at his beard. "First, they can catch mice more efficiently and cheaply than any traps. And second, like the secret room and the documents, they'll really make Wardour feel like a place with a fascinating past."

Mrs. Hapgood frowned slightly but said nothing.

Dr. Adam went on. "Mrs. Hapgood, don't you think your guests would be delighted to meet the cats that are a living link to the famous ones from the past?"

Mrs. Hapgood looked down at the little family. "I suppose you have a point there," she admitted. "Maybe people will be interested in seeing some real cats as well as those documents." She paused. Mandy held her breath. And then came the words that Mandy had waited so long to hear. "The cats can return to Wardour," Mrs. Hapgood announced at last.

Mandy felt as if she were going to explode with relief. "Fabulous!" she cried out, grinning at James.

"Real cats!" Joanne said, breathless with excitement.

"A good decision, Mrs. Hapgood." Dr. Adam smiled at the hotel owner. "And I'm sure you'll love them once you get to know them. Cats have a way of working themselves into people's hearts!"

"Well, I don't know about that," Mrs. Hapgood said hastily. "I just hope they're healthy."

"We can tell you that right away," said Dr. Emily, picking up one of the tabby kittens and examining it.

Mandy's dad did the same. He chose the ginger one that looked so much like Puss and checked its ears, eyes, and mouth. The little animal squirmed vigorously and mewed as Dr. Adam lifted its tail. He smiled and replaced it next to its mother. "A nice, healthy little female," he said confidently. "Although she's a bit underweight."

Then he examined the mother. "Her coat's very dry and she's terribly thin," he commented. "She's not in great condition. But it's nothing that some decent food and a warm bed won't fix."

With all six cats checked thoroughly and given a clean bill of health, it was time to take them to their new quarters. Mandy picked up the mother while the others carried the kittens. James handed Mrs. Hapgood the ginger one that looked the most like Puss. Mandy felt a rush of relief as Mrs. Hapgood held it gently and stroked its furry head. The little kitten looked up at her and opened her mouth wide in a tiny, high-pitched mew.

"They'll have to sleep in the scullery," Mrs. Hapgood said firmly as they made their way down the ladder. "I don't want them wandering all over the place."

Mandy smiled to herself. Mrs. Hapgood would have to learn that cats slept anywhere they pleased!

The cats were greeted with cries of delight from the other guests at the door of the barn. To Mandy's relief, Mrs. Hapgood looked pleased by their enthusiasm and began to point out the similarities between the ginger kitten and the pictures of Puss that appeared in the castle.

As they began to make their way back across the stubbly field, Mandy turned and looked back. The building looked cold and empty, but the faintest of breezes whispered around its walls. And then above the breeze came the sound of laughter — a joyful peal that rang out across the fields. Mandy looked at the guests. No one else seemed to have heard it. Mandy smiled. She was sure it was Joe, laughing with delight now that his precious Puss's descendants were going back to where they belonged.

The cat and her kittens were soon safely installed in the scullery in a cozy cardboard box. Mandy and James left Joanne filling a bowl with tasty chicken scraps and joined the others in the drawing room. Fellows was serving cups of tea and slices of Mrs. Moore's cake.

Mrs. Hapgood greeted them with a smile. When Mandy and James each had their snacks, she tapped her teacup with a spoon to attract everyone's attention. "Well, in all this excitement, has anyone managed to solve the mystery?" she asked.

To Mandy's complete surprise, James jumped up. "I have!" he declared. "The gardener stole the candelabra, then he hid it in the chapel."

"Absolutely right!" said Mrs. Hapgood, sounding almost as astonished as Mandy. "How very clever of you!"

Dr. Adam looked stunned. "How on earth did you come up with the right answer when you were so busy with everything else?" he wanted to know.

James pushed his glasses down his nose and peered out over the top of them. "Elementary, my dear Dr. Hope," he joked.

When the loud laughter that met James's remark died down, he explained how he had worked it all out. "You see, when we met the gardener yesterday, I noticed he was wearing heavy boots," he told them. "And last night, we were in the chapel and I saw a candleholder on the altar."

"But altars often have candleholders on them," Mr. Russell pointed out.

"I know," said James. "But this one was more like the candelabra I noticed in our information pack, and it looked much more ornate than anything else in the chapel. I thought it might be a really good hiding place for the stolen property, as long as no one looked too closely."

"And then?" Dr. Emily prompted. "What made you decide it was the gardener who put it there?"

James looked uncomfortable, as if he weren't sure how much of their midnight adventure to reveal. Mandy nodded at him encouragingly, so he took a deep breath and continued. "Well, Mandy and I heard some strange noises while we were in the chapel, and when we went outside, we saw someone behind a gravestone. When we went to investigate, I noticed a footprint that looked like a heavy boot had made it," James explained. "So I put two and two together and guessed we must have surprised the gardener when he was putting the cande-labra on the altar."

Mandy shook her head in admiration. "Typical James!" She smiled warmly at her friend.

"Or just plain lucky," Dr. Adam teased.

A movement at the door drew Mandy's attention.

Joanne was standing there. "Mrs. Hapgood," the young girl began shyly, "Mom and I have settled the cats in the scullery."

"Thank you," said Mrs. Hapgood. "Just as long as I don't have to feed them," she added with a dry smile.

"Oh, you won't," Joanne reassured her eagerly. "I love looking after them." She caught Mandy's eye and a broad smile spread across her freckled face. Her curly red hair gleamed in the sunlight, and she looked hap-pier and more excited than Mandy had ever seen her.

Mandy stared at the little girl and caught her breath as something suddenly hit her. Joanne looked just like Joe! Why hadn't she noticed it before? Then Mandy re-membered what Mrs. Hapgood had told them on the first evening. Mrs. Moore's family had worked at Wardour for many years and she was the great-niece of a former cook, Mary. And, according to what Fellows had told them earlier, Mary was Joe's sister!

Mandy did some rapid calculations in her head. Then she nudged James. "Do you realize?" she whispered to him happily. "It's perfect for Joanne to look after the cats! She's Joe's great-great-niece!"

Look for the next Animal Ark™ book:

HUSKY IN A HUT

"That was a gun!" Mandy gasped. Beside her, Okpik flinched and whined. But Nanook seemed unaffected by the sinister noise. She leaped forward at the sound of the shot, yanking her leash right out of Pani's hand. Then she sped down the snowy slope and vanished behind a large rock.

"Nanook, come back!" shouted Pani. "I couldn't stop her!" she cried miserably to Gaborik.

"After her, quick!" said Gaborik. He set off at a run, the other huskies bounding in front of him, their ears flat with alarm.

Mandy slipped and slid in the snow behind Gaborik as she raced to keep up. "It's all right," she said over and over again, realizing she was trying to convince herself as much as the terrified huskies.

A high-pitched yelp sounded somewhere ahead of

them. "Nanook," Pani whispered, fearing the worst as they rounded the rock to where her dog had last been seen.

Ahead of them was a shallow gully. Huddled together to their right were Tom Ellison and Ben Page. The men looked terrified. One rifle lay discarded on the icy ground, but Mr. Ellison was pointing his in the air. The wisps of smoke coming from the barrel showed that he had fired the shot they had heard.

Mandy followed their horrified gaze and stopped dead in her tracks. Just a few yards away from them was a huge wolf. From the tracks in the churned-up snow, there had clearly been many more here. Perhaps the others had been frightened away by the gunshot. But this wolf remained, snarling, its tongue flicking over its sharp, pointed teeth as it glared at the two men.

Mandy's heart sank when she saw that Nanook was standing between the wolf and the men. The husky was staring at the wolf curiously with her wide pale eyes. Unlike the other huskies, her fur lay flat along her back, and she didn't seem scared at all.

"Everybody keep very, very still," Gaborik commanded in a low, clear voice. "If the wolf thinks you're going to attack, it might try to get you first!" One of the huskies he was holding was Sedna. She began to growl threateningly, and he shushed her.

"Oh, please come back, Nanook!" Pani sounded close to tears. "Please, girl!"

"I've got a flare gun in my pocket," Gaborik told them. "I'll fire it in the air and scare the wolf away."

"But you might scare Nanook away, too!" Pani cried.

Mandy gazed helplessly at Nanook and the wolf. While Nanook was sleek and muscled, the wolf was lean and hungry looking, with matted, unkempt fur that was dirty white with distinctive charcoal-colored smears. Its eyes were cold and yellow and narrowed at Nanook and the two men. It bared its teeth and started to growl.

"I'll show the wretched thing," muttered Mr. Ellison. He lowered his gun and squinted along the barrel.

"No!" Mandy cried. She saw the wolf tense itself, ready to spring.

Gaborik raised his hand to gesture to Mr. Ellison not to fire. But at the same moment, Sedna tore her leash free of his grip and sprinted bravely forward.

Before it could turn, the wolf tumbled backward under the husky's fierce attack. The two creatures snapped at each other, kicking up flurries of thick snow.

To Mandy's horror, she saw that Mr. Ellison was still preparing to shoot. "Stop! You could hit Sedna!" she yelled.

Gaborik thrust the leashes of the remaining dogs into Mandy's shaking hands and ran toward the two men.

Mr. Ellison looked up in surprise to find the burly Inuit man bearing down on him. A moment later, he and Ben Page went down in a heap as Gaborik cannoned into them. The rifle spun through the air. To Mandy's relief, it landed in the snow without going off.

But Sedna and the wolf were still fighting.

"Back, Sedna!" Mandy shouted. "You've scared it enough, let it go!"

Sedna showed no signs of having heard. Her jaws were clamped on the wolf's back. It kept twisting its head and snapping back at her, but it couldn't reach. Every time it tried to twist free it only managed to drive Sedna's teeth farther into its skin.

Then Nanook charged into the fray.

"Not you, too, Nanook!" cried Pani in despair. "Come back! Leave the wolf alone!"

But it wasn't the wolf Nanook was lunging for, teeth bared. It was Sedna. With an angry howl, Nanook launched herself at the other husky, biting at one of Sedna's hind legs. The bigger dog let go of the wolf, confused to find herself coming under attack. The wolf stumbled clear, lurching toward Mandy and Pani and the rest of the dogs.

"Keep away!" Mandy shouted, yanking the dogs closer to her.

The wolf stared at her for a moment before shaking its massive head, as if clearing its senses. Then it turned and pounded away, vanishing into the dusk.

Meanwhile, Sedna was snarling with rage, her jaws scissoring at Nanook's muscular flank, teeth tearing at her fur.

"Stop!" Pani yelled. "Stop fighting, you two!"

Gaborik waded in between the two fighting dogs, trying to separate them. Without thinking, Mandy shoved the dogs' leashes into Pani's hands. Then she skidded down into the gully, her only thought to pull the two dogs apart.

"Keep back, Mandy, it's dangerous!" Gaborik said through gritted teeth.

But Mandy had seen Nanook's terrified eyes as the husky realized she'd picked a fight she couldn't win. Mandy held out her arms to Nanook, trying to draw her away by her collar, but her gloves made her clumsy. She pulled them off and slipped freezing fingers down between the cold leather strap and hot, wet fur. She felt Sedna's teeth scrape against her arm and was grateful she had the thick padding of her parka for protection.

At last, Gaborik had a proper hold on Sedna and pulled her away. He looked up at Mandy, and his eyes flashed with anger. "You foolish girl," he said to her as he stroked and soothed the frantic Sedna. "You could've gotten yourself badly hurt!"

Mandy looked at him in surprise, blinking away the tears of fear and relief that were threatening to come. Nanook was whining softly, her head in Mandy's lap. "But I couldn't just stand here and let them hurt each other."

Gaborik's angry face softened. "Apparently not."

Pani came over with the crowd of dogs and threw her arms around Mandy. She was shaking all over. "You were so brave, Mandy, but you shouldn't have done that."

Mandy hugged her back, then took a deep, shaky breath. Okpik pushed forward to Nanook, sniffing her anxiously. She was breathing deeply and quickly, her eyes only half open, her ears flattened against her head.

"It's all right, girl," Mandy told the husky. "It's all over now."

"Is she hurt?" Gaborik asked.

"I — I'm not sure," Mandy said. "I think she could be in shock."

"Why would she attack Sedna like that?" Pani wondered, gazing down at Nanook with worried eyes. "It looked as if she was trying to protect the wolf!"

"I don't know what she was doing," Gaborik admitted. He whistled through his teeth. "Just don't scare me like that again, old girl!" Then he swung around to face Tom Ellison and Ben Page, who were painfully picking themselves up from the icy ground. "And that goes double for you two!"